F
McDonagh, Margaret.
A game of love   18.99

A GAME OF LOVE

Annabel needed to get away, to take stock of her life. But her holiday got off to a dismal start; whilst driving through France she gave an English couple a lift, and they repaid her by making off with her car and possessions! Fortunately, a handsome Frenchman stopped to help. He showed Annabel nothing but kindness, but when she realised he was the ex-tennis player Alain Ducret, who had the reputation of a playboy, she fought to resist falling for his charms . . .

*Books by Margaret McDonagh
in the Linford Romance Library:*

MARGARET McDONAGH

A GAME
OF LOVE

Complete and Unabridged

LINFORD
Leicester

First published in Great Britain in 1997

First Linford Edition
published 2000

British Library CIP Data

McDonagh, Margaret
 A game of love.—Large print ed.—
Linford romance library
1. Love stories
2. Large type books
I. Title
823.9'14 [F]

ISBN 0–7089–5918–0

Published by
F. A. Thorpe (Publishing)
Anstey, Leicestershire

Set by Words & Graphics Ltd.
Anstey, Leicestershire
Printed and bound in Great Britain by
T. J. International Ltd., Padstow, Cornwall

This book is printed on acid-free paper

For Mum — forever missed,
forever loved, and for Dad —
father and friend beyond compare.
In memory of blue seas, blue skies,
happy days, mosquitoes . . . and
Hurricane Hortense!

1

The squeal of tyres biting into Tarmac had Annabel Smith spinning round from admiring the panoramic view in time to see the car slew sideways, straighten, then vanish round a sharp bend.

'Hey!' she yelled, running along the twisting road. 'What do you think you're doing?'

Realising the futility of her words, she stopped and planted her hands on her hips, directing a scream of angry frustration at the French mountains. For someone who was reputed to be discerning and self-possessed, she had been remarkably gullible. To think she had believed the English couples' sob story and had offered them a lift. Instead, she was the one who had been taken for a ride.

Denise — if that really was her name

— had been crying quietly at a table in the café where Annabel had stopped for lunch, and the boyfriend, Charlie, was comforting her, a worried expression on his face. Realising she was English, they had confided in her, told how they had been deserted with no money and only a smattering of French between them.

They had been desperate to get to Nice to meet up with Denise's parents. So desperate, it seemed, that they had left her in an even worse situation than the one in which they had claimed to be.

Giving vent to her temper, Annabel kicked at some loose rocks on the roadside, scuffing the toes of her trainers. It had all been a con and she had been too blind and trusting to see it.

And now here she was on this lonely, mountain road, her only possessions the clothes she stood up in — a skimpy, denim bikini top, cut-off shorts, her trainers and a floppy straw hat. And her camera . . . the camera she had grabbed when she had left the car to take a photograph of the spectacular view.

Everything else, all her luggage, maps, money, credit cards and her passport, were in her car — the car that at this moment was careering down the mountain with two confidence tricksters inside. The only evidence that remained was the rubber marks left by their getaway.

How could she have been so stupid? She had felt sorry for them, and it had been good to talk to fellow Britons after three days alone on the road from Calais journeying down through eastern France. They had both been younger than her twenty three years, and she had been concerned for them and way of them hitching at the roadside, even as a couple. You heard such awful things these days.

A humourless laugh escaped. She was the victim here. Stranded in the early evening, what remained of her schoolday French pitifully inadequate, with perhaps a very long walk to some kind of habitation and assistance. Annabel took a moment to look around her and assess her situation. There were two choices — up or down. She glanced behind her at the steep gradient of the mountain. OK, so she'd go down.

She couldn't remember how far it was round this spur until she could rejoin the main road, but standing still was not going to bring aid any closer. With a sigh of resignation, she began the tedious walk downhill.

The sun was warm on her skin. It was late spring. May would soon give way to June, and although she imagined the flowers were past their prime, they had been beautiful in their variety and colour. Melted water still swelled the cascades and torrents that had carved their way through the mountainous rock over countless centuries.

But the scenery that had captivated her previously that day, deep, narrow gorges, wide river valleys, Alpine pastures, woods of chestnut and pine, the roaring mountain peaks of the Pre-Alps, now appeared daunting to her, unfamiliar, overwhelming. She

4

knew no-one, did not even have the most basic of maps to guide her.

This holiday had seemed like a good idea at the time. At least, Annabel amended, she had allowed others to persuade her it was. She tilted back her straw hat and squinted at her surroundings, anxiety at her predicament clenching like a fist inside her.

A gentle breeze stirred wisps of the shiny, straight blonde hair that framed her delicate face and hung down to her shoulders. The soft and flyaway strands were the kind of colour that Robbie had frequently said reminded him of ripening corn on a clear, summer day.

Annabel sobered as her thoughts lingered on Robbie. Dear Robbie, her childhood sweetheart. They had shared so many dreams, planned their future with excitement and hope. He was the only person she had ever been out with, the only man she had kissed, the only man with whom she had ever envisaged sharing the rest of her life.

Fifteen months ago, they should have

been married. They had planned it, anticipated it, saved for it. Fifteen long and lonely months since that day, two weeks before the wedding day, when Robbie was late leaving work and had raced to meet her to view a possible house for them to live in . . . the day Robbie had been killed in a car accident . . . the day Annabel had felt her life had stopped as well.

For a long time she had not wanted to go on. But her family, and all her friends, had cajoled and bullied her through one day at a time.

She would never forget Robbie and would always have a special place for him in her heart. But as time passed and daily life gradually became easier to endure, she had worked like a demon in the bookshop, had begun to see her friends again, had found she could even laugh again. She had also visited places she and Robbie had been to together and remembered more of the good than the bad. But she would never forget the happiness and love they had shared.

It had been her friend and business partner in the book shop who had been most vociferous in her insistence it was time Annabel take a holiday. Samantha had said she must go away, alone, experience new places, new people, have the space to think things through in her own mind.

The truth was that she had been working too hard, way too hard. Ten weeks ago, at the point of exhaustion, she had suffered acute appendicitis. The effects of Robbie's anniversary so recently passed, the anaesthetics and pain relief she had been given, and her general rundown state, had combined to make her weepy and listless. The stress had finally caught up with her.

It was a sign she had taken notice of. Now was a time to stand back and take stock, to make choices about her life before she drove herself into the ground. And the time had come when she wanted to fight, when she wanted to live after all.

Robbie was gone. It was painful, but nothing could bring him back. It was over, the dreams gone. She could either falter or she could carry on.

Annabel knew what Robbie would have wanted. She also knew she had the love and support of her family and friends who had seen her through the last fifteen months. Unsure as yet what she could expect from the future, even the direction she wished to take, she had to admit she was feeling better, more at peace inside herself.

Already she had more colour in her cheeks, a healthy glow to her skin, and her blue eyes that had been dulled by pain and grief were more vital and brighter than they had been in a long while.

And so she had packed her bags, hunted out her passport, and pointed her car in the direction of Dover and the cross-Channel ferry. The drive through France had been pleasant, the hours alone giving her the time and space Sam had suggested she needed to rebuild her goals.

But now, what was supposed to have been a gentle convalescence of both mind and body, a regathering of her physical strength and her mental resolve, had turned into a nightmare.

The sound of a car engine cut through her reverie, and she stepped to the side of the road and turned to watch as a beaten up van appeared round a corner. Annabel sighed with relief and raised a hand to flag the driver down.

The vehicle never slowed in its downward flight, and Annabel gaped in angry disbelief as the driver ignored her yells and waves for assistance and soon disappeared out of sight.

She let out a curse of frustration. Goodness only knew how long it would be before another car came along, and when it did, there was no telling the driver would stop. What was she going to do?

Annabel glanced at the watch Robbie had given her for her twenty-first birthday. At least she had not lost that precious possession. She sighed when she saw the time. It was nearly three quarters of an hour since she had been stranded. By the time she was able to reach some sort of civilisation and report what had happened, the two thieves would have had a considerable start and be long gone. They could go anywhere — through France, or over the border into Italy or even up towards Switzerland.

Gritting her teeth, Annabel stepped back on to the road and continued downhill. It could not be too long before she reached the main road and surely then someone would stop to help her — if she could make herself understood.

Then she would need to report what had happened, after which it would be necessary to find somewhere to stay . . . difficult with no money of any description and no form of identification.

As soon as possible she would have to telephone the credit card company, and her bank to report the stolen travellers' cheques. There was also her stolen passport, driving licence and her missing car. On top of which, she had to break the news to her parents that she was stranded.

With the beginnings of a stitch pricking her right side at the unaccustomed exercise after her enforced rest following her operation, Annabel forced herself to keep putting one foot in front of another.

She glanced up in concern as the sky clouded over. With barely any warning, a short but violent shower soaked her to the skin before she could take cover beneath an overhanging rock.

Her straw hat flopped limply on her head, drops of water cascading from the brim. Annabel shook her head. Lady Luck was not smiling on her today. She managed to protect her camera from the worst of the rain, and then, as rapidly as it had begun, the shower eased, chased away by the breeze.

As the sun returned to bring light

and shadow to the early evening, Annabel resumed her walk, hoping she did not look so drowned and pitiful that a potential rescuer would think twice before coming to her aid.

Her spirits lifted a short time later when, glancing down after a bend in the road, she saw the glint of the sun on glass and metal. Cars! Yes, there between the rocks and the trees, she could see traffic.

Annabel breathed a sigh of relief. Not far now to the main road. She could make it. Buoyed at the prospect of an end to this nightmare, Annabel quickened her pace.

2

Annabel stood on the southbound side of the main road disappointed to find that the traffic was sporadic.

Despite her predicament, her natural caution was making her uncomfortable about what she was attempting to do and wary of the necessity of placing herself in the care of a stranger.

A lorry had slowed down for her, but she had taken one look at the two scruffy, heavily-bearded men in the cab and decided she could not bring herself to go with them. It may have been unfair, and she may only have imagined the lascivious grins on their faces, but she was not prepared to take that chance.

But she would have to take a chance some time, she decided a few moments later, biting her lip in frustration. She could not stand here all evening, and nor could she hold out in the hope of a patrolling police car. There was nothing for it but to fight her indecision and take the plunge.

The next two cars that passed both avoided her as she stepped off the verge, the drivers ignoring her arm-waving signals for them to stop. Annabel glared after them and muttered her annoyance.

Fresh anxiety warred with her frustration and caution, and she determined that come what may, the next vehicle would stop or run over her in the effort to pass by.

At the sound of a deep, powerful engine approaching, Annabel gritted her teeth, closed her eyes, and stepped out on to the Tarmac. A horn blared, and she peeked beneath her lashes as a menacing black sports car drew nearer. Surely it was going too fast?

Her heart pounded, and whether it was fear or stubbornness that rooted her to the spot, Annabel was unsure. She only knew that she couldn't move. At what seemed like the very last moment, the engine note changed and the car rapidly decelerated, pulling off the road and on to the verge beside her.

Sucking in a steadying breath, Annabel forced her shaky legs to carry her to safety at the roadside. Once there, she rested a hand on the sleek bonnet, feeling the reflected heat from the engine beneath. Before she could gather her nerves or admire the graceful lines of the Ferrari, a masterpiece of Italian engineering, the driver's door opened.

She watched with the faintest flicker of alarm as a body unfolded itself from the low-slung car — a very masculine body. That the very masculine body was clad in an expensive, biscuit-coloured suit, a white shirt, and a slightly-askew toned tie, made an impression immediately.

It was his face, however, that caught her attention the most. Tanned and angled, a five o'clock shadow darkening the determined jawline, it was a face that encompassed far more than the surface, film star good looks, hinting at a humorous personality and a strong character.

In his early thirties, he was lean and attractive, a few inches taller than her own five foot eight. Her assessment of him was completed in a few silent seconds, then as he stepped towards her, his dark eyes narrowed with annoyance, Annabel blinked and battled the desire to retreat from him.

He ran well-shaped fingers through his short, thick hair, velvet black like the midnight sky, and then he frowned, beginning a tirade in rapid, angry French. Bemused, Annabel stared at him. She recognised an occasional word of what was clearly a Gallic dressing down.

The dark gaze swept over her, and she was conscious that her hair felt damp and lank, that her clothes were skimpy and untidy, and the straw hat that remained perched on her head was fit only for the dustbin.

When he finally ran out of words and gazed at her with a mixture of impatience and expectancy, she licked her lips and gave him an apologetic smile.

'Parlez-vous Anglais?'

For a split second he looked thrown.

'You are English, mademoiselle? You are in some kind of trouble?'

'Yes, yes, I am. Please, can you help me?'

'But of course,' he allowed, his expression softening. 'Tell me what has happened.'

His English was fluent and his voice, warm, husky and with a lilting accent, sent a shiver down her spine. Thankful for the opportunity to explain her situation, Annabel set her awareness of the man aside and told him of the events of the afternoon and the predicament in which she found herself.

The man frowned as he listened to her story, his dark eyes filled with sympathy and concern. He leaned against the car, his arms folded across his chest, a faint pout of consideration on his disturbingly sensuous lips.

'OK,' he nodded as she finished her explanation. 'We will go to the nearest police station and make the report, yes?'

'Thank you.'

'Please, you will get in the car.'

A smile accompanied his invitation, a smile that robbed her of the power to move for several seconds. He ought to have a licence to look at someone like that, she thought, heat curling inside her.

There was a distinct possibility any mortal woman would melt at his feet. She shook her head. What on earth was wrong with her? Had the afternoon's upsets addled her brain?

Fighting for composure, Annabel jerked away from him, disturbed when he followed her round the car and politely opened the passenger door for her. She murmured her thanks and slid inside with as much grace as she could muster. Her gaze followed his progress round the front of the car and back to the driver's door.

He slid behind the wheel, the door

closing them in together, and Annabel bit her lip, uncomfortable at a feeling of claustrophobia. Her awareness of him heightened as he glanced at her, his disturbing gaze trailing over her from her dishevelled hair over her bare midriff to the long expanse of bare leg. She had the irrational feeling it was like a physical touch.

When his gaze finally rose to meet hers, the expression in those smouldering dark eyes was enigmatic but a touch of male appreciation shone through. Wariness returned. She was taking a risk, knew nothing whatsoever about this man except that he was well-dressed, drove an expensive car and would grace any magazine or silver screen the world over. None of which was any safeguard. Was she being too trusting again?

'What is your name, mademoiselle?' he asked after a moment of silence.

She gave a start, her nerves tense.

'Annabel Smith.'

'Annabel . . . '

The way he said her name in that huskily-accented voice raised goose-bumps on her skin.

'And you?' she queried, hoping that her voice reflected none of her inner turmoil.

'I am Alain Ducret.'

A frown tugged her brow as he looked away from her and switched on the engine. As it hummed to powerful life, he checked the rear-view mirror and then pulled back on to the road.

Alain Ducret.

The name sounded vaguely familiar to her but she was at a loss to know why. One thing was certain, she allowed as she flicked a surreptitious glance at him from beneath her lashes, he was not the kind of man any woman would forget.

He intercepted her gaze and sent her a ghost of a smile.

'You are nervous, yes? You are wondering now if it was such a good idea to step out into the road and make me stop.'

'I . . . ' Her words faltered.

'For all I know, Annabel, you may be doing to me what you say the young couple did to you,' he pointed out and gave a Gallic shrug. 'I take the same risk, no, in coming to your aid?'

Annabel found herself smiling back at him. It was impossible not to. And he was right. It was an act of trust for him to believe her tale and offer to help her. she had not thought of the situation from his point of view.

She looked at his strong profile as he concentrated on the road, learned the clean-cut lines and angles of his face, the shape of the shadowed jaw. Her gaze settled on the lean, attractive hands that kept a light but sure contact with the steering-wheel, effortlessly controlling the powerful car.

Dragging her gaze away, she leaned back in the seat and closed her eyes, tiredness creeping over her. The low purr of the engine lulled her, and yet all her senses were aware of Alain's presence beside her. Even the car's interior held a faint but potent tang, a trace of leather, the aroma of man, some lingering of a subtle, musky aftershave.

'So, Annabel, you come to France on your own, and yet you do not speak any of the language?'

Her eyes flicked open. The way he had expressed his comment made her holiday sound wild and reckless.

'Women do travel alone in this day and age, Monsieur Ducret,' she replied, prickling in defence at his apparent criticism.

'Of course, but I think perhaps you are not so worldly-wise, hmm?'

Even though charm and amusement were reflected in his voice, Annabel fumed. He made her feel gauche and unsophisticated, and her dishevelled appearance only added to the picture he must have formed of her.

It was on the tip of her tongue to tell him she was perfectly capable of taking care of herself, but she bit off the retort just in time. Had she been more worldly-wise, she would not be in this fix in the first place.

Disgruntled, she turned her head away from him and stared out of the window, blind to the passing scenery as she frowned over her thoughts.

'Annabel?'

Her name on his lips and the light touch of his hand on her arm roused her from a doze. She looked about her, realising they had stopped.

'Where are we?'

'The gendarmerie. Come, we explain your misfortune.'

Inside the building, her nervousness increased as they waited for someone to attend to them. Alain smiled in encouragement as they were shown into a small interview room by a young officer. After a few moments, a rotund, grey-haired official entered, a smile of recognition creasing his weathered face as he saw Alain.

'Monsieur Ducret!'

Annabel watched with some bemusement as the young officer's eyes widened with apparent disbelief. The ebullient, older policeman chattered rapidly to Alain for some moments, but then his gaze turned to her. He raised an enquiring eyebrow and directed a question to her she did not understand. She glanced at Alain for guidance.

'Annabel, this is Inspector Bonneau. He will take your statement.'

As Alain smoothed over the language problem, translating the inspector's questions and relaying her answers, Annabel was both surprised and thankful for his presence and assistance.

The young officer, restored to calm efficiency after studying Alain for some minutes with silent awe, tapped out the official report on an antiquated type-writer as Annabel gave them all the details she could about her stolen possessions and the young English couple she had tried to assist.

Alain helped her with all the formalities, gave her moral support, even arranged for a drink of juice for her.

She would not have managed to

make her situation clear without him, and she could only wonder at his patience, his willingness to devote so much of his time to help her.

Nor could she help but wonder who he was. The reaction of the officials to seeing him stirred her interest. Clearly Alain was someone respected and recognised even in this small, country town. Her gaze rested on his relaxed figure as he sat, legs crossed, on one of the hard, wooden chairs.

The more she looked at him, the more something about him was vaguely familiar. She just could not pinpoint why his name had rung a bell.

He turned his head, his gaze intense as it met hers, and she battled against the heat that threatened to stain her cheeks.

'Do you want me to read the statement back to you, Annabel?' he queried, the fingers of one hand absently releasing the button at the collar of his shirt.

'Thank you.'

Annabel tried to concentrate on his

words, but she was captivated by the sound of his voice, the way his mouth moved when he talked. When his gaze flicked to her face once more, Annabel looked away, and forced her wayward mind to focus on the important matter at hand.

Her statement signed, a copy of the report neatly folded and consigned to the pocket of her denim cut-offs, Annabel thanked the policemen for their friendly assistance and stepped back outside. The sun was beginning to descend behind the western hills, and the air was beginning to cool.

She turned round and saw that Alain was still in conversation with the inspector. Although both men glanced at her from time to time, she could neither hear nor understand what they were discussing.

Finally, Alain shook the man's hand, and stepped outside to join her. As they walked together towards Alain's car, Annabel's footsteps slowed.

'What is the matter, chérie?' Alain

asked as he opened the passenger door.

Annabel glanced up at him in sudden confusion. With the formalities completed, it was just dawning on her that she had no money, no means of getting home, nowhere to stay.

'Annabel?'

She hesitated and did not get back into the car. What was she doing blindly following Alain? He had delivered her to the police, had discharged his promise, she could not impose on his generous nature any longer.

'I am grateful for all that you have done,' she told him, her voice laced with tension. 'But I should stay here until I decide what I should do next.'

Alain smiled, that smile that weakened her knees.

'This has all been arranged, and I have given the inspector my details. Where else are you to go, Annabel, but home with me?'

3

'You're not serious?' Annabel exclaimed in shocked amazement at Alain's suggestion.

'But of course I am serious,' he responded as if it was the most natural thing in the world. He spread his hands in a Gallic gesture of appeal. 'What other options do you have, chérie?'

Annabel hated to admit that she could not immediately think of a single viable alternative. But to go with Alain, to stay at his home? Caught in an agony of indecision, she cast a glance back towards the police station. The inspector, it seemed, was content to turn her over to the care of this man. Surely that must count for something?

However, her misgivings remained. She returned her gaze to Alain and met the warmth of his dark brown eyes. Had her reluctance more to do with her confusing and unwanted reaction to him than to any recognisable fears for her safety?

'I have to contact the consulate, my bank, the credit card company,' she attempted to offer by way of excuse.

'It will all be taken care of from my home.'

'But — '

'Do not worry, chérie, you will be safe and cared for.'

Still Annabel hesitated, unwilling just to hand herself over.

'I can't put you to this inconvenience.'

'My housekeeper will be delighted to see you. She is very strict with me, and I would be in considerable trouble if she found out I had abandoned you here. You do not want that, do you?' He gave her a disarming smile. 'Please, Annabel, allow me to help you.'

Taking her silence for acceptance, Alain persuaded her, unprotesting, into the car. Soon he was beside her, the throaty engine revving as he pulled away and drove through the small town, heading south.

After translating for her at the police station, Alain now knew all about her; where she lived, what she did, all her personal details. It made her feel vulnerable, especially as she knew nothing about him. A frown creased her brow. Who was Alain Ducret? And where exactly where they going?

As if he sensed her restlessness and the questions that were forming in her mind, Alain smiled across at her.

'You are wondering about me perhaps, Annabel? It is all right for you to ask me whatever you wish to know.'

'Your name was familiar from the beginning,' Annabel admitted, hoping he would not think her rude. She looked at him but saw only amusement in his eyes. 'I'm sorry, I feel I should know, but . . . You're famous, aren't you?'

He shrugged slightly, as if his notoriety was of scant importance to him.

'Once I was infamous, maybe!' he

conceded with a husky chuckle.

'In what way?' she asked, intrigued by him.

'Are you interested in sport? No? Perhaps that is just as well or you would really be nervous of me and my fearsome reputation.' He laughed at the doubtful expression on her face. 'I was the wild boy of the tennis courts, but do not worry, chérie, my really wild days are over!'

Memories surfaced, snippets of news and articles and stories she had heard about him in the past.

'Of course! But you look different.'

'I think that is age,' he commented with a wry smile as he slowed down to negotiate a road junction. 'It is many years ago that I stopped playing tennis, a long time since I was a name worth column inches in the newspapers. Now I have my private life to myself.'

Annabel did not want to dwell too long on thoughts of what that private life might be. She did not need to be a sports fan to have heard about the reputation he had spoken of, the trouble he had allegedly been in, the trademark pout and stormy personality, the tales of parties and women.

It was hard to believe this was the same man. Was he really so different, or had the stories been exaggerated to sell papers? She watched him from beneath her lashes. He seemed so natural, so down to earth and easy to be with. Was that instinct right, or was Alain Ducret a wolf in sheep's clothing?

Not a comforting thought. Yet she remained intrigued by him, and the underlying excitement and electrical charge she experienced in his presence was disturbing.

'I have been in Switzerland today attending to some business,' Alain continued after a few moments. 'It is lucky for you I visited my family near Grenoble and took this route home, yes?'

'Yes. I am really grateful for the trouble you are going to.' Annabel smiled.' Where is your home, Alain?'

'I have lived for some years in Monte Carlo. Have you been there?'

'No, never.'

She had heard of it, of course — the playground of the rich and famous with its world-renowned casino and celebrated Royal family. It was a world far removed from her own, Annabel allowed with concern, and glanced down at her scruffy, inadequate clothes with a wry grimace.

'Monaco is very beautiful, chérie, and I hope that you will enjoy it.'

'I am sure I will,' she replied politely, hoping she had hidden any trace of her inner doubts.

Alain glanced across at her and caught her picking at the frayed hem on one leg of her old, denim shorts.

'Do not frown so. Tomorrow we will go shopping.'

'Oh, but I can't, I — '

'Please, allow me the indulgence, Annabel,' he cut in, waving her protest aside. 'It is a selfish thing to find that it brings me pleasure to assist you.

Besides, you will need some things before your bank can arrange some replacement money for you.'

Annabel stifled a further rush of refusals. There was no use arguing the point at the moment, she decided. Instead, she would cross that bridge if they came to it tomorrow and find a tactful way to refuse his offer.

For now, as Alain concentrated on the road ahead, and the glorious colours of a wonderful sunset played across the sky, Annabel relaxed back in her seat, her thoughts on the man at her side.

There were so many things she wanted to know about him. Why had he walked away from his life in tennis when from what she had heard, he had been at the peak of his form and ranked high on the world list? What did he do now? What was this business he had mentioned that occupied his time and energy? Had he really been as wild and disreputable as the tabloid Press had claimed?

Since he had rescued her from the

roadside, he had been nothing but kind and gentle. Contrary to his remarks, he was not in the least selfish, but had been generous in every way with his time and assistance. A tiny inner voice began to ask the uncomfortable question . . . what may Alain want or expect in return?

'Why are you helping me, a total stranger, this way?'

She had not meant to voice the query aloud, but it slipped out just the same. Annabel turned her startled gaze towards him. In the dimming light inside the car, she thought she detected a twinkle of mischief in his eyes.

'You think that after the legendary antics of my youth that it is unlikely that I have become so respectable?'

'I'm sorry, I didn't mean . . . ' Annabel felt her face colour with discomfort.

'I tease you, chérie,' he relented with a soft laugh as her words trailed off and she looked at him with anxiety. 'Why did you come to the aid of the young

English couple who robbed you?'

'I was concerned for them. I could not just walk away and leave them when I believed they were in trouble,' she explained.

Alain responded with a smile.

'Then you will understand this was the same for me also?'

'Yes, I understand, but . . . '

'Please, Annabel, you must not fret about this being a problem for me. Just accept, all right?' he insisted, as he identified the anxiety she failed to hide. 'We have just passed the village of La Turbie,' he continued, turning the car down a steep and twisting road. 'Look down now. Even in the growing dark, Monaco is spectacular, no?'

Annabel's breath caught in her throat as she took her first sight of the fabled Principality. Guarded within the shelter of the mountains, the shoreline was brushed by the calm warm waters of the Mediterranean.

From the lofty vantage points as Alain negotiated the hair-raising road,

Annabel gazed at the luminous, irides-
cent lights, the reflections on the
surface of the sea.

'It's magnificent,' she allowed, her
voice barely more than a whisper.

As they came closer, Annabel admitted Alain was right about the night-time
effect, but she longed to see it all in
daylight. It was one of the most
picturesque sights she had ever seen.

Despite her tiredness, her anxiety at
the loss of all her possessions, and the
uncertainty of her immediate future
having accepted Alain's hospitality, she
felt a building excitement.

'My villa is in a little road off the
Boulevard d'Italie towards the eastern
end of Monte Carlo. We will be there
very soon,' he promised as they
descended into the Principality and
followed a one-way system. 'In the
morning, you will have a lovely view
over the houses and between the coastal
hotels to the sea.'

In a matter of minutes, he was
turning off and driving up a narrow

road. He pressed a button inside the car, and a large pair of wooden gates swung open between two solid, brick posts. Lights on the outside of the villa allowed her to form a first impression.

Square and substantial, it was in the same style of many others they had passed, creamy yellow on the walls and with a reddish roof. As the gates closed behind them, Alain halted the car in front of a double garage off to one side of a short, curving drive that looped a large and ornate fountain.

As they left the car, the front door of the villa opened, and a tiny, white-haired woman stepped out to meet them, a smile on her face. She nodded to Annabel in friendly greeting and then posed a couple of rapid questions to Alain in French. Alain answered her briefly, then drew Annabel forward with a hand at the small of her back.

'Annabel, this is Cecile Florent . . . my nanny!'

Alain grinned as the elderly woman tutted crossly at him.

'Take no notice of him, Annabel. He has been giving me this cheek since even before he learned to walk! Now, please, you must come in and let us make you comfortable. I am so sorry to hear of your trouble,' she finished, her English less fluent, her voice more accented, than Alain's.

Inside, the villa was beautiful. Annabel hesitated in the vast hallway, looking around her in amazement. The central hall was square, and all the doors on the ground floor led off it. There was a single, wide staircase directly opposite her that led to the upper floor, and she could see that a gallery ran all the way round.

It seemed that the predominant colour was white, even the marble floor, but splashes of colour in the form of paintings or ceramics, pots of green plants and vases of flowers, saved it from starkness.

'What a beautiful home you have.' She smiled at Alain.

'I am glad you like it. Come to the

living-room and you can make your telephone calls.'

Alain provided her with the codes and the phone, and left her to report her stolen money and cards to the out-of-hours hotlines. She discovered that the consulate was closed until Monday, nor could she expect any replacement cash until after the week-end. It looked as if she would have to impose on Alain's generosity for two more days.

Last of all, she placed a call to her parents, giving them an edited version of events. Wary of mentioning Alain, and uncertain of her immediate plans, she promised to ring them again when she had more definite news.

When she had finished her calls, Cecile appeared as if by magic and offered to show her to her room. She followed the housekeeper up the wide staircase and along the upper gallery, almost gasping aloud as she was shown into a large, plush and beautiful room.

As with the rest of the villa she had

seen so far, the basic colour was white, but in this room, there was a dusky pink carpet, deep and soft. A delicate quilt covered the bed, pure white with embroidered pastel flowers that matched the pattern on the curtains that fringed the floor-length windows that led out on to a balcony. Annabel was enchanted.

'This is lovely, Cecile, thank you.'

'You are welcome. Your bathroom is through this door,' she informed, indicating to one side of the room. 'Please, take your time, and when you are ready, come down and I will prepare something for you to eat.'

For a few moments after Cecile had gone, Annabel stepped out on to the balcony. The air was fresh and clear in the dark of evening and she enjoyed the feel of the breeze against her skin as she looked at the lights, the play of moonlight out on the deep water.

Back indoors, she undressed and went to the bathroom to take a shower. The water felt good against her skin, and she used the toiletries provided to wash the residues of her travels from her body and luxuriated in the easing of some of the tension from her muscles. The scar from her operation was fading nicely, and she hardly noticed it now, except if she did too much or was over-tired.

She washed her hair, then towel dried the flyaway blonde strands until they were soft and silky round her face. Wrapped in a towel, she went back to the bedroom. For a moment she lingered, then she gave in to the temptation of her tiredness and lay down on the bed for a few moments. She would indulge in a brief rest, then she would dress in her one shabby outfit and return downstairs.

Annabel stirred from her doze feeling disorientated. Light spilled in from the gallery, and she was aware of the open door, of a human shape nearby. Just as she was about to move, to speak, she heard a husky whisper of a voice speak softly in French. Annabel frowned, not

42

understanding what was being said.

'Alain?' she asked hesitantly, hearing a soft exclamation in response.

'I did not mean to disturb you,' he apologised, stepping closer and looking down at her, his expression hidden by the shadows. 'I have brought something for you to sleep in.'

'Thank you.' Annabel took the offered silk shirt, holding it against her. 'Alain, what did you say?'

He gave a short laugh and brushed a wisp of hair back from her face.

'Do not trouble yourself about it. Maybe one day I will tell you. Now, you are tired. Sleep. We will talk again in the morning.'

Annabel sighed as his fingers trailed softly down her cheek, disappointed when the touch was withdrawn. Burrowing down in the comfortable bed, she gave herself up to sleep, a smile on her face as her mind filled with the image of a tall, dark, handsome Frenchman.

4

Sun filled the bedroom when Annabel woke the next morning. She could not remember when in the night she had tossed the damp and rumpled towel aside and pulled on the cream silk shirt Alain had loaned her, but the fabric felt wonderful against her skin. As she turned her face to the collar, she could smell a lingering, musky trace of Alain.

Annabel rolled over in the bed and stretched lazily, then reached out a hand to take her watch from the table. Her eyes widened when she saw that it was almost nine o'clock. She had slept for hours.

Slipping from the bed, the hem of the shirt slid down her legs almost to her knees as she walked towards the open windows where the curtains swayed gently in the soft, morning breeze. She stepped out on to the balcony and leaned on the railing, trying to absorb the beauty of the view.

All around were assorted villas and blocks of apartments. Below her, between houses, she could see an attractive church, and lower still, between a couple of tall buildings was the sweep of the Mediterranean. She had never seen such a colour. The water, rippling and sparkling under the sunshine, was the most incredible bright azure.

For several moments, she gazed about her, mesmerised by her presence in their fairytale place, then a light tap on the bedroom door claimed her attention. She returned to the room in time to greet Cecile who entered carrying a tray laden with breakfast.

'Bonjour, Annabel, I hope you slept well.'

She beamed, setting the tray on the bed.

'Good morning. Yes, I slept too well, Cecile! I am sorry that I did not come down again last night.'

Cecile smiled aside Annabel's concerns.

'Not at all, ma chérie. You were tired after your upsetting day. But you are hungry, n'est ce pas?'

'Breakfast looks lovely, thank you.'

'Then I will leave you to enjoy it.' Cecile smiled, stepping towards the door. 'Alain is doing some work in his office. When you are ready, he asks that you join him. Turn left out of your room and go around the gallery to the third door.'

When the housekeeper had gone, Annabel turned to her breakfast with relish. There was a plate of warm croissants, assorted mini jars of jam, a glass dish with curls of butter, a glass of orange juice and a pot of coffee.

She lingered over her meal, unwilling to admit she was nervous at the prospect of seeing Alain. The previous evening was a vague memory. She had been sleepy and had most likely imagined the warm intimacy of his voice when he had spoken to her, the heat of the touch of his fingers against her face. She wondered again what he had said to her in French and wished she could understand.

Her breakfast finished, she washed and dressed in her cut-off shorts and denim bikini top, feeling displeased with her appearance. Sucking in a deep breath, she left her room and followed Cecile's directions to Alain's office.

As she approached the third door, she could hear Alain's voice, and realised he was speaking not in French, nor English, but Italian. Annabel wondered how many languages Alain could speak with such fluency.

The door stood open, and as she hovered in the entry, her gaze settled on Alain. Dressed in dark trousers and an open-collared cream shirt, he was leaning back in a leather chair, his feet propped on the corner of his desk. Finished in burgundy leather, it was strewn with files and papers.

She watched him as he talked on the telephone, his free arm hooked behind his head. His dark hair was ruffled and untamed, his jaw shadowed with a day's growth of beard. He looked rakish, dangerous, and even more attractive than she remembered.

As Alain dropped his feet to the floor and altered his position to reach a notepad and pen on the desk, he saw her. Annabel's heart did a curious flip-flop when he smiled and beckoned her into the room.

'I will be a moment,' he promised, inviting her to a comfortable, soft leather sofa by a west-facing window with a wave of his hand.

While she waited for him to finish his conversation, she glanced discreetly round the office. Furnished with the desk, chair and sofa, it also housed several large filing cabinets, a large table and several chairs, and one large area of shelves on one wall containing various box files, reference books and what looked like catalogues of some description.

A few photographs in silver frames occupied odd nooks and crannies, and mostly they appeared to be family portraits, Alain with an older couple and two other men about his own age. She realised there was nothing depicting his days on the tennis circuit, no photographs, no trophies.

She turned her gaze to admire the view of the Principality from the window, half her mind wondering once more what Alain's business was. It was a Saturday, and yet he was deep in conversation on what appeared to be a work-related matter.

At that moment, he laughed, the warm, rich sound arresting her attention, and she turned her gaze back to him as he finished his call and hung up the receiver.

'So, the sleepyhead awakes,' he teased as he stood up and crossed the room. 'I trust you had a comfortable night?'

'Yes, thank you. I'm sorry I was so rude and fell asleep.'

'Do not apologise. I understand.'

He seemed younger and more relaxed than ever this morning, the cream silk shirt setting off the darkness of his jaw and his tanned skin. His eyes were warm and sparkling with life as he sat beside her and smiled.

'So, I am all yours . . . for the weekend at least! We have much to see and do, but first I think we need to buy you some more clothes.'

'But — ' She bit off her protests as Alain frowned at her.

'Annabel,' he chastised, 'I thought we had settled this yesterday. You cannot spend all your time in one outfit until your affairs are organised.'

Annabel bit her lip feeling over-whelmed by his forceful personality and continued generosity. Without giving her time to formulate further arguments, he took her hand, stood up and drew her to her feet.

'Come, we are ready to go. I will show you the rest of the house later.'

Feeling weak-willed, Annabel allowed Alain to usher her downstairs to the waiting Ferrari. She settled in the passenger seat, watching the wooden gates swing open before Alain drove out and down to the Boulevard d'Italie.

'We will drive round and see something of Monte Carlo first, yes?'

Annabel nodded, eager to have the opportunity to explore before she left this enchanting place. She remained silent, absorbed in looking out of the window as Alain negotiated the traffic and pointed out things of interest.

Her first impression was how clean and well-maintained everything was, from the swept and orderly streets and pavements to the mass of vegetation, the palms, shrubs and flowers that were lush and healthy.

'Much of this land has been reclaimed from the sea,' Alain told her as he turned on to the avenue that ran along the section of coast she had seen from her balcony that morning. 'People are surprised there is so much here when the Principality is so small, smaller even than Hyde Park in London.'

Annabel was surprised also at the

number of buildings and roads that were stacked on the hills. She turned her head and looked over the white beach at the radiant blue of the sea and along the curve towards the oddly-shaped building that stretched over the shore.

Alain drove through the tunnel beneath the building which he told her was a hotel and conference centre, and as they exited into daylight once more, she had her first view of the harbour below the Rock of Monaco where the palace sat proudly.

All around and behind the ranks of buildings, the mountains rose in a sheltering arc, the rocky hillsides brushed with shrubby vegetation. She returned her attention to the harbour.

Within its arms, clusters of white yachts rode the gentle swell at their moorings. Some craft were small, some were more like ships, and one, to her amazement, even sported a car and a helicopter on its stern.

Alain smiled at her reaction and her

pleasure in her surroundings.

'I will be your guide for the next few days. We will be tourists. There is so much more to Monte Carlo than gambling and a car race, as you will see.'

Annabel smiled back at him, but she was unwilling to be drawn on his assumption that she would stay that long. Aside from the question of imposing on his hospitality, she was not at all sure it was wise to allow herself to remain. Being near Alain was beginning to arouse all manner of confusing sensations inside her, sensations she was anxious to ignore.

Before long, Alain parked in the town and they walked a short distance to a boutique. Just from looking at the outside Annabel could tell it was far too expensive and her apprehension increased.

Either Alain was unaware of her hesitation or he chose to ignore it. His hand was firm and disturbing on the strip of bare skin at her back as he opened the door of the shop and guided her gently inside.

He greeted the smiling, young woman who emerged from the rear office with a kiss on both cheeks, and then he stepped back, drawing Annabel to his side as he explained her predicament in French.

Annabel did not want her wayward mind to linger on the fact that Alain was well-known here, nor that maybe he often brought women here to shop. This was entirely different from that kind of thing, she assured herself. But as she glanced around at the clothes and noticed some of the prices, she nearly fainted. She could never afford to buy anything here.

'Annabel,' Alain murmured, his husky use of her name drawing her startled attention. 'Chantal speaks a little English, so I will leave you together to decide what you will need.'

'I really don't think this is a good idea,' she whispered to him.

He tutted, his fingers beneath her

chin raising her gaze for his inspection.

'Don't be silly. You cannot wear only your little top and shorts . . . as delightful as you look in them,' he added with a mischievous grin.

Annabel felt hot all over from his appraisal and the feel of his touch on her skin. Flustered, she stepped away, breaking the disturbing contact. Aware of Chantal's presence, Annabel stifled her discomfort, and unwilling to make a scene or appear unappreciative of Alain's efforts on her behalf, she reluctantly held her tongue.

Alain nodded his satisfaction at her apparent agreement.

'So, I will see you soon, chérie.'

After he had left, Annabel was shown around the small and select shop, and then Chantal gathered several garments from the rails and left her in the fitting room to try them on. Her intention to accept only the bare necessities was soon swept aside as Chantal was clearly under instruction from Alain and overrode all Annabel's protests.

By the time they had finished, Annabel was seriously concerned about the expense. Feeling as if she had been picked up and shaken by a whirlwind, she sat on a chair in the discreet waiting area and stared in some confusion at the parcels stacked beside her.

Along with underwear, there were a couple of T-shirts, a pair of designer jeans, a shaded green sundress, canvas shoes, evening sandals, and a simple but flattering black cashmere dress that alone cost more than a busy Saturday's takings at the bookstore.

Her bikini top and cut-off shorts had been discarded and packed out of sight, and she sat now, sipping the coffee Chantal had brought her, in a light-weight, sleeveless dress that left the creamy curve of her shoulders bare, and a full skirt that swirled around her legs.

As Chantal attended to another customer, Annabel sat back to wait for Alain, and idly flicked through some French fashion magazines on the small glass table beside her. At the bottom of the pile, she uncovered a leatherbound folder with the logo of Chantal's boutique embossed on the front.

Curious, Annabel opened the folder and found it contained transparent pages filled with cuttings and articles about Chantal, her work and her boutiques. Written in several languages, Annabel discovered from reading an American piece that Chantal designed many of the clothes on sale in her select boutiques, and although small, her business was successful and her designs sought after by fashionable women the world over.

She was about to close the folder when the picture at the bottom of an article from a French newspaper caught her eye. She looked at it more closely. No, she had not been mistaken. It was Alain . . . and he had his arm around a tall, thin woman. Dressed in an immaculate, dark suit, an enigmatic smile on his face, he looked devastatingly handsome.

The woman was turned towards

Alain, leaning into him, so her features were indistinct, but from her profile, Annabel could see she looked beautiful, the sumptuous evening gown she was wearing setting off her slender frame.

The picture was black and white which made it difficult to form an impression of her colouring, but her hair was clearly too dark for blonde and yet nowhere near as dark as Alain's.

Annabel wished she could read the article, but the only part that stood out for her was the caption beneath the picture — **Alain Ducret avec Yvette Lachaud**. There was no date on the cutting, but from Alain's appearance and his short hair, she guessed it was taken within the last few years.

The tight knot of disappointment that formed within her at the evidence of Alain's involvement was uncalled for, she rebuked herself. From the moment she had known who he was she had been aware of the stories about him, and he was far too handsome and

58

charming a man to be without female company. Nor did she have any wish to feel anything about him at all apart from gratitude for his assistance.

As the door of the boutique opened and Alain strode in, Annabel closed the folder with a twinge of guilt that she had been prying, and set it back under some magazines on the table. Fighting down her inner deflation, she became conscious of the boxes beside her and began to worry once more.

Alain smiled in approval as he looked over her appearance, and after a brief conversation with Chantal, he began to gather up the parcels.

With a brief smile of thanks to the young woman who had watched over her with friendly firmness, Annabel followed Alain to the waiting Ferrari, and watched as he stowed the items inside.

'What are you worrying about now, chérie?' he asked with some amusement as he turned to face her and saw her anxious frown.

'I can't allow you to buy these things for me.'

With a dramatic sigh, Alain placed both his hands on the roof of the car either side of her head. As he leaned closer, Annabel felt crowded by his physical presence. Her breath quickened, her pulse raced. Their gazes held.

'The cost is insignificant to me, so there is no need for your concern . . . as I have already told you.'

'But — ' Her protest trailed off unformed.

Alain's dark eyes watched her discomfort, and a small smile played around his mouth.

'You are wondering if there is something I want from you in return?'

Annabel froze, every nerve ending aware of him, his closeness, the subtle fragrance of musky aftershave. Alarmed, she placed her hands on his chest in an effort to maintain at least some distance between them. Beneath her fingers she could feel the warmth of his skin through the silk of his shirt, feel the steady rhythm of his heartbeat.

'Alain,' she murmured, her voice a mere whisper, as fear built inside her that he was going to kiss her — fear because she recognised with inner shock that a wayward part of her wanted him to do just that.

'Do not be afraid of me,' he murmured back, the husky timbre of his voice affecting her even as his words were meant to reassure. He moved a hand, the fingers tracing around the outline of her jaw before passing softly and slowly across her parted lips. 'I take nothing from anyone that is not freely given.'

At the precise moment that Annabel was unable to prevent herself from swaying towards him, Alain released her and stepped away. For several moments, Annabel tried to gather her scattered wits. She realised that Alain had opened the passenger door for her and was waiting with his customary solicitousness for her to get in. Annabel forced herself to comply.

She was silent on the journey back to his villa, her mind occupied. Alain was dangerously exciting, vital, physical, and he raised her pulse in a most disturbing way. But she had to maintain her guard. She had always considered herself self-avowed, confident, even mildly sophisticated.

But being with Alain for less than twenty four hours made her realise she was still naïve in the ways of the wider world, his world, certainly in dealing with other men on a personal footing.

In the past, Robbie had always been there. They had been a couple. She met other men from being involved with someone else, and so there had been no question of anything other than friendship or business, certainly no interest on her part for any man other than Robbie.

Now, alone these past months since he had died, she was having to learn about being single, about interacting with men from a different position . . . as a lone woman and not part of an established couple.

And what of Alain? Was Yvette, the woman in the picture, still a part of his life? If not her, then someone else . . . were his playboy days far from over?

Annabel glanced at the man beside her. She was rather afraid that Alain was far too much for her to handle.

5

'What a beautiful room!' Annabel crossed the threshold into the library at Alain's villa and gazed in delight at shelf after shelf of books.

Unlike the rest of the villa which was modern and spacious, the library was old-fashioned, designed by someone who adored books and who had created the perfect ambience of casual comfort to aid relaxed enjoyment to learn or lose oneself in the pages of a classic or modern novel.

'Of course, chérie, books are your work, yes?'

Annabel nodded in response to Alain's question and smiled back over her shoulder at him as she walked towards one wall of shelves, crossing the oriental rug that covered the polished wood of the floor.

'I have always loved books since I was

64

a child,' she told him now, the nervousness that had stayed with her through lunch now evaporating. 'It was like a dream come true for me to find the bookshop.'

'And who looks after your business while you are away?' Alain queried, moving to lean against one of the inviting sofas.

'Sam, my partner.'

'Sam?'

'Mmm. We run the bookshop together.'

Annabel found a section of English books and tilted her head to study the titles.

'Actually, it was Sam's idea I take this holiday. The last year or so has been difficult for me, and after my operation . . . '

Realising her tongue was running away with her, Annabel straightened and looked at Alain. Grim disapproval shadowed his face.

'This man . . . ' he began.

Annabel frowned. 'Excuse me?'

'Sam, you said . . . ' He broke off as

Annabel laughed. 'I do not find it funny that your Sam is so irresponsible that he sends you off alone to a strange country when you are still recuperating from surgery.'

'Sam is a girl — short for Samantha,' she explained, hiding a grin.

Comprehension dawned in Alain's dark eyes, and something that looked for an instant like relief, but it was gone before she could be certain.

'Now I understand. All the same, chérie, to travel alone so soon.'

'I'm fine. My doctor was perfectly happy for me to come on holiday.'

Alain watched her, a frown of concern pulling his brow.

'What was wrong that you needed an operation?'

'My appendix,' she told him. 'A routine matter these days.'

Alain was silent for several moments, but she felt his gaze on her as she browsed along the shelves.

'And is there a boyfriend waiting anxiously at home for your return?' he asked, his voice warm.

'No.'

'I have made you sad,' he stated contritely. 'What is it, Annabel?'

Again she turned to face him, her thoughts on Robbie.

'I was to be married, but he was killed in a car accident.'

Even now her voice wobbled as she explained the ending of her dreams, her happiness, with the loss of Robbie.

'Chérie, this is tragic. I am so sorry.'

'Thank you.' Annabel's gaze locked with his. 'It happened over a year ago.'

'And you have shut yourself away?'

'Not really.'

Annabel moved around the room to peruse another wall of books and evade his probing gaze. She had shut herself away, of course. It was one of the reasons she had come on this holiday, to try to sort out her feelings and plan for an unexpected and unwanted future alone. But she did not feel comfortable sharing her insecurities with Alain.

She glanced at several rows of books

in various foreign languages.

'Just how many languages do you speak?' she asked, raising a querying eyebrow at her host.

'Six with some fluency,' he admitted, watching her with amusement.

'Six!'

He folded his arms across his chest and laughed.

'I can get by in another one or two.'

'Show off!' She looked along the shelves and counted them off on her fingers. 'French, English, Italian, what else?'

'German, Spanish and Russian.'

Annabel let out an envious whistle.

'It must be wonderful to have an ear for languages. I never mastered it and always regretted that I never persevered.'

'Do not regret. To regret is to waste time and experience,' Alain admonished gently, walking towards her. 'You can always learn.'

'I tried with French at school, but . . . '

'But?' Alain raised an eyebrow.

'Our teacher was not inspiring and I had other interests at the time.'

'Say something for me.'

'What?'

'Something in French that you remember.'

She blushed and stumbled over a few words before stopping.

'I can't. You'll laugh at me.'

'No,' he promised, a twinkle in his eye. 'Your accent is good. You must try to speak more.'

'I could never master all the masculine and feminine verbs.'

She shrugged, backing away, embarrassed.

'You still have a problem with the masculine and feminine?' he queried with a teasing smile as he took hold of her hand and prevented her retreat. 'We shall have to see what we can do to sort out these misconceptions of yours while you are here! There is much that I can teach you.'

'You would find me a boring student,' she excused, freeing her hand from his disturbing touch, fearing that whatever Alain expected to teach her, she could not afford to learn.

'I doubt that, but time will tell. And speaking of the time,' he continued with a smile, allowing her retreat this time. 'We shall spend the afternoon exploring the sights, yes?'

'I'd like that.'

Relieved to break the tension that had been building between them, Annabel preceded him out of the library and into the marbled hall.

'Come,' Alain said as they left the house and crossed the driveway. 'We will walk and enjoy the fresh air and the sun.'

Annabel was happy with the suggestion and was eager to see and discover all she could in the short time she would have in Monte Carlo. They walked along the Boulevard d'Italie until they came to the Carmelite church she could see from her balcony, then Alain took her hand and led her down a long flight of stone steps, through a small tunnel, descending until they emerged near the beach.

Annabel was enthralled with the fairytale location. They followed the curve of the seashore, through the stand of trees, until they came to the tunnel they had driven through that morning. It was all so beautiful, and although it was so far apart from her own world, she felt comfortable and relaxed, strangely at home here.

Alain was wonderful company. He was knowledgeable and enthusiastic, and despite her awareness of him, he was easy to be with and had a dry sense of humour. When they arrived at the harbour complex, he showed her the marks on the road from the recent Grand Prix and the chips in the walls where the cars had come a little too close for comfort.

He took her first up to the old town of Monaco on the Rock. She took many photographs of the Palace from the cobbled esplanade, then Alain took her to the balustrade to see the view over the port of Fontvieille.

'Have you seen the cannons, Annabel?'

he asked, leaning against the wall and smiling at the absorbed look on her face. 'See how the pyramids of cannon-balls are cemented to stop the tourists from removing one and collapsing the whole arrangement.'

They had missed the changing of the guard through the entrance with the coat of arms above, but two stood in their dark uniforms at the twin red and white sentry boxes.

'Can we go inside?'

'I am sorry, chérie, it is not open at the moment.' He ran a finger down her cheek at her crestfallen expression. 'But there is much else we can see.'

Alain rested his hand at her waist and guided her away towards the more modern but still beautiful cathedral. They looked around for a while and walked past the resting place of Princess Grace.

'She was so charming and serene,' Alain whispered close to her ear. 'Very much missed here.'

Back outside, they wandered through

the narrow streets of the old town, browsing in shops where Annabel chose postcards to send home. She was surprised by the maze of streets, at how much was in such a small place.

Lastly, Alain took her to the Oceanographic Museum. It was an impressive and imposing building that seemed to rise straight up from the sea out of the rock on which it stood.

They spent hours inside, and Annabel was fascinated by all the exhibits, the explorations and the species of marine fauna in the Aquarium.

'Am I asking too many questions?' she worried as they walked to another section of the museum. 'This must be very tedious for you.'

'Not in the least. Your enjoyment makes me happy. You make it all fresh and exciting, as if I, too, am seeing it all for the first time.'

'You are very kind.' Annabel blushed at his compliment.

'I only tell the truth,' he stated, linking his arm through hers. 'You have breathed new life into me.'

They moved on from one exhibit to another, and throughout it all, Annabel was increasingly conscious of him, her reaction to him. He was a physical man. He liked to touch and be touched in a way that was instinctive and unconscious.

Her own family was an affectionate one, her childhood having been filled with warmth, cuddles, hugs of greeting and comfort. She was used to that, to an arm draped around her shoulder or her waist.

But from Alain, it took on a new importance, heightened her awareness of him. Each touch fired her blood in a way she found disturbing because it had been a long time since anyone had roused interest in her.

Since Robbie, she had not imagined she would be able to feel anything again. However much the physical contact may be a mere gesture meaning nothing to Alain, she was concerned by her reaction to him.

That her emotions could be beginning

to awake as if from a long and numbing sleep was scary. She was not at all sure she was ready to cope with their re-emergence, not here, not now . . . maybe not ever.

Most of all, Annabel knew that she could not let Alain's kindness, his attention, his experience, and this romantic setting turn her head. If she was not careful of her emotions it would be all too easy to come headlong out of the vacuum and make a very big mistake.

6

It had been an enjoyable but busy weekend, Annabel reflected as she sank on to the sofa in the library with a contented sigh.

Perhaps she was becoming too contented. A faint frown pulled her neatly arched brows as she watched Alain cross the room to pour them each a night-cap. True to his word, he had been the perfect host. She already felt comfortable in his home, and whilst much about him remained a mystery, she had come to like him more and more as the hours with him slipped by.

Although they had talked a great deal, especially about books, music, the theatre — all interests they shared — and although Alain was generous with his time and his hospitality, he revealed little of his inner self to her.

Not that she should be surprised,

Annabel acknowledged as Alain removed the stopper from a crystal decanter of brandy. After all, she was a guest in his home through unfortunate circumstances, not through any personal desire of his for her company or friendship.

He was being polite and doing his duty while she was in his care. That was all. It was a shock just how much disappointment that admission engendered within her.

His smile warmed her as he crossed the room and handed her a glass.

'To you, chérie,' he murmured, clinking his own glass against hers, his dark eyes enigmatic as he sat beside her.

'Thank you for this weekend, Alain. I've really enjoyed myself.'

'It has been my pleasure.'

A warm glow filled her as she met the intensity of his gaze. Disconcerted, she glanced away, cupping her fingers round her glass as she took a small sip of her drink, her body aware of his nearness, her mind on him and the time they had shared together.

Their sightseeing on Saturday had been followed by a delicious meal prepared by Cecile and eaten in the villa's beautiful dining-room. She had been tired after their packed day, and had enjoyed the remainder of the evening curled up on this very sofa reading in companionable silence while Alain went through some papers he had brought down from his office.

Sunday had followed a similar pattern. They had left the villa after a leisurely breakfast and driven along the coast towards Nice, stopping along the way at Cap Ferrat to look at the splendid exterior of the pink-hued palace of the Rothschild foundation and its gardens.

After lunch in Nice, they had explored the village of Eze on the way back to Monaco, and Annabel was still in awe of the way the houses and narrow streets hung from the mountain slopes.

That evening, despite her protests,

Alain had persuaded her to change into the black cashmere dress she had acquired from Chantal's boutique the previous day, and he had taken her to a local bar where they had joined some of his friends.

She could vividly remember her initial hesitancy and shyness of a few hours ago, but instead of feeling an outsider and excluded by language, she had soon been accepted and made to feel at ease by the group.

What explanation Alain had given for her presence in his home, she had not ascertained. But over drinks and a light meal, she had begun to relax, drawn out of herself by the friendly conversation and laughing as she had not done for many months.

The only sour note had come when she had excused herself to visit the powder room. She had heard the outer door open and shut, then one woman greeted another. Annabel remained hidden feeling both guilty and upset as she overheard their conversation.

One of the women was American, the other had a European accent she could not identify. Neither had been in her social group that evening.

'Did you see that Alain Ducret came in with someone tonight?' the American asked.

'I did. Who is she, do you know?'

'I have never seen her before.'

'I wonder what Yvette will say when she hears Alain has a new playmate,' the other commented with a wry laugh.

'I can imagine there will be fireworks!'

Silence followed for a minute, and Annabel hardly dared to breathe.

'There was a rumour that Yvette was seen with someone at a Paris night-club last week.'

'Yvette? That'll be the day!' The American laughed. 'Does Alain know that?'

'I cannot say. I have not spoken to him in a while — I would not be foolish enough to ask!'

Both women laughed again, and

Annabel heard signs of their movement towards the door. Then the American woman spoke again.

'Let's hope that Yvette keeps away from Monaco for a while.'

'You think she will come back when she hears?'

There was incredulity in the question, and again the response was wry.

'Yvette always comes back.'

There voices trailed off, and the outer door swung shut behind them, leaving Annabel alone with her thoughts. For several moments, she waited in the powder room as she attempted to smooth her ruffled composure.

Alain's reputation was such that she was already being viewed as his latest playmate! The realisation did not sit well. Her questions about Yvette and her place in Alain's life intensified.

That unsettling incident had been a couple of hours ago, and she had not found the nerve or the opportunity to ask Alain about Yvette. She was a guest in his house because of his generosity in her trouble . . . she was not a friend. It was not her place to question his private life, and she did not wish to risk a rebuff.

Now it was late and she was alone with Alain in his villa. Lost in her thoughts, she started when his fingers trailed softly down her bare arm. Her gaze shot back to meet his.

She did not remember him being quite that close — certainly his arm had not been resting along the back of the sofa, a hair's breadth from her shoulders. Her elemental awareness of him continued to increase until her skin seemed to tingle.

His eyes smouldered and she felt flickers of heat prickle along her nerves in response. Her gaze lingered on his face. She had not realised before how thickly lashed those dark eyes were, nor that his mouth was so tempting.

Alarmed at her wayward thoughts and too conscious of his closeness Annabel scrambled to her feet with more haste than dignity. Her fingers tightened around her glass as she took a hasty swallow of the brandy, then she set it aside.

As she walked across the room, her legs shaky, she could feel his gaze on her every step of the way. She sucked in a steadying breath, then trailed the fingers of one hand across the spines of the English books that occupied one of the shelves in front of her.

'May I borrow one of these while I'm here?' she asked, unable to resist a glance back at Alain over her shoulder.

He swirled the brandy in his glass and watched her, his expression enigmatic.

'Of course, chérie, by all means help yourself,' he invited with a small smile as he set down his own glass on the table and rose to his feet with cat-like grace.

Annabel ignored the quiver of alarm at his approach and forced herself to return her attention to the selection of Thomas Hardy novels that had captured her interest. She had read them all in the past, but she removed one from the shelf now and clutched it protectively against her chest before she turned round.

Alain was so close she felt almost pinned to the bookshelves by his sheer magnetic presence. Her pulse raced as his fingertips traced the outline of her jaw, their touch seeming to sear her skin.

'Alain . . . ' she murmured helplessly.

'Sssh.'

He was going to kiss her. Her breath locked inside her as he closed the last of the distance between them. The first touch of his lips on hers was whisper-soft, teasing, tempting.

Even as she told herself to pull away from him while she had the chance, in only a matter of seconds the battle was lost, and she sighed her acquiescence, her surrender, against his mouth.

An eternity after it had begun, the book forgotten and her fingers clenched in the fabric of his jacket, a warning bell sounded in her head and finally managed to permeate the haze that enveloped her. What was she thinking of? She was mad to be reacting to Alain in this way.

She knew of his reputation, suspected that he may be involved in some way, if not with the mysterious Yvette, then with someone else. With a super-human effort, she dragged herself away from him and sucked much needed air into her parched lungs.

His breath fanned her heated cheeks, his eyes smoky and intimate as he looked down at her. For a moment she was almost grateful that his arms were so tight around her as her knees felt rubbery and quite unable to support her. Then, with a burst of determination, she pushed against him and wriggled free of his embrace.

Her heart thudded noisily against her ribs, and she licked her expertly-kissed lips, tasting a trace of brandy, the sweet tang of Alain. Green eyes wide with nervous alarm, she glanced up at him.

'I'm sorry,' she murmured, her voice sounding strange and husky to her ears.

'I can't do this.'

She was not ready, for any man, especially one as complex and disturbing as Alain with all his past and his unsolved mysteries. Disappointment and reluctance were reflected in his expression, but he didn't make any attempt to touch her again or change her mind. Instead, he folded his arms across his chest and regarded her flustered countenance, a hint of a smile curving his mouth.

No! She did not want to so much as think about that mouth. His smile faded as, flushed, she backed away from him.

'You are afraid of me?'

Annabel heard the surprise and concern in his voice.

'No, but . . . '

'But?'

'It's just that I — ' She hesitated, searching for words, unwilling to confess she was scared of the way he made her feel. She was more afraid of herself than of him, afraid he could make her forget her reason. It was all too intense, too soon. 'I'm confused at the moment. And since Robbie . . . '

A frown pulled his brow as her explanation trailed off. His dark gaze searched her face. Then he gave a Gallic sigh and stepped towards her, the fingers of one hand smoothing a few flyaway strands of hair back from her face, his touch reheating her skin.

'You need time, chérie?'

Annabel offered a smile and a murmur of consent in reply, knowing as she did so that her time in Monaco and with Alain was almost over.

'We will take things slowly,' he allowed, a sudden smile bringing a teasing devilment to his eyes. 'And I will try to be a gentleman.'

She should have felt reassured by his promise, but somehow she didn't. Alain was a very sensual man, and, she suspected, not a very patient one.

Amusement bright in his eyes, Alain bent down and retrieved the book that had slipped to the floor during their explosive kiss. Was he laughing at her? She must seem gauche and unsophisticated to him, Annabel groaned, overreacting like a dizzy schoolgirl. Feeling awkward and a touch piqued, she accepted the book from his outstretched hand, her gaze averted.

'I have an appointment in Milan tomorrow that I cannot cancel,' Alain told her as she was about to turn towards the door. 'I would like to take you with me, but with no passport this is not possible. I am sorry.'

'That's quite all right. I have my own affairs to organise.'

He smiled in response to the brisk edge of independence in her voice and inclined his head with mock gravity.

'Of course. Make yourself at home here, and I will see you for dinner.'

'Good-night, Alain.'

'Good-night, chérie,' he teased softly, a chuckle rumbling from his chest as a faint blush tinged her face. The husky, accented voice followed her to the door. 'Sweet dreams.'

Upstairs in her room as she prepared for bed, she replayed the evening in her mind. Alain had been such good company, and in the couple of days she had known him, he had filled her thoughts to the exclusion of everything and everyone else, overwhelming her with his generosity, his personality, and his attention to her needs and well-being. No matter that she had only known him for such a short time. Being with him felt good — too good.

And now he had kissed her with Gallic flair and hot passion. She felt disloyal, guilty, confused, because while enjoyable and loving, Robbie's kisses had never excited her to the kind of feverish desire she had experienced in Alain's arms a short while ago.

What she had shared with Robbie had been deep and gentle. Their lifetime friendship had moved to affection and respect, and then to love. There had been a special closeness, the comfortable familiarity of a secure and loving future together, but none of the wild electricity that scrambled her senses whenever Alain looked at her, touched her.

She did not need to be a sports enthusiast to have heard stories of his past wild and disreputable reputation. If the stories of his private life had been true, he had loved and left a string of beautiful women.

She did not even want to think about the temptations he must have had, the tennis groupies, the women he had known. He had looks and charm, and whilst she was not influenced by his jetset lifestyle and his wealth, many would be. He could pick and choose his female company, so why was he turning his attention on her?

And what of Yvette? Clearly they had been, or were, a couple. She did not like to listen to gossip, but she had been unable to help overhearing the conversation in the powder room that evening.

He would have her believe he had left the old Alain Ducret, the renowned playboy, behind when he gave up tennis, but after tonight she wondered if that part of him had disappeared completely. Again she wondered why he would seek to woo her, an ordinary English girl, when he met so many glamorous women.

Fate had brought her here, but her stay in Monaco would be brief, and she and Alain were nothing more than passing acquaintances, an unfortunate victim and the good Samaritan who had offered his help.

Annabel slid into bed and plumped up the pillows, unwilling to focus on the stab of disappointment she felt. Where was her commonsense? It had not been much in evidence since she had met Alain, but she had better smarten up if she did not want to make a fool of herself.

With a sigh, she gazed out of the window past the fluttering white drapes at the midnight, star-filled sky. It was so beautiful here in the fairytale Principality, and it would be all too easy to lose her head if she wasn't careful. Tomorrow she would attend to her business, sort out her money and her passport, and then she would have to say her goodbyes.

She swallowed the sudden lump in her throat and turned over. It was no good pretending things could be any different than they were. The sooner she pulled herself together, banished any foolish notions, and returned to her own life in England the better.

7

When Annabel went down for breakfast
the next morning it was to discover that
Alain had long since left for Italy. Cecile
was busy with household tasks, and so
Annabel lingered over her breakfast of
croissants, jam and coffee, lost in
thought.

Despite her resolutions the night
before, it was hard to imagine leaving
this place. She had been enchanted
with the villa and its setting from the
moment she had arrived, and on top of
that was her confusion over her
awareness of Alain.

Even in sleep, her wayward mind had
still been filled with him, his image
haunting her dreams. It was another
sign, if she needed it, that she must
bring this interlude to an end.

First thing after breakfast, and after
checking with Cecile, Annabel went to

the sun-filled living-room, L-shaped and sumptuously decorated, to telephone the British Consulate. The nearest office, she discovered, that attended to lost and stolen passports, was way down the coast at Marseille.

'You may stay and finish your holiday if you wish,' an official told her. 'When you require an emergency document to get you back to England, bring a photograph to this office and we will arrange it for you. It would be best to telephone again first. Will you be flying home?'

'I hadn't thought that far. I suppose I shall have to.'

'Well, some airlines and French Immigration may accept the police report and allow you to travel. The E U should help you there. You could check with them at Nice first.'

Thankful that her repatriation should not prove a major problem, Annabel completed her call. Next she turned her attention to her finances. After talking to her bank, she found they had received word of her difficulties, and replacement funds and travellers' cheques would be available for collection at a nominated bank in the Principality that afternoon.

Although she had no identification, they were faxing her signature and documentation, and she had the police report as additional verification. Satisfied, Annabel went in search of Cecile.

She found the friendly Frenchwoman in the roomy, well-equipped kitchen cleaning items from a large silver canteen service with painstaking care.

'May I help you?' Annabel asked.

For a moment Cecile hesitated, but reading the appeal in Annabel's eyes, she smiled and inclined her head.

'I would enjoy your company, ma chérie.'

Annabel sat beside her and followed her lead, cleaning the pile of spoons Cecile placed before her. Several minutes passed in companionable silence, then Annabel's curiosity bettered her.

'You said you had known Alain since he was a boy, Cecile.'

'All of his thirty-two years. I was housekeeper for his mother before any of the children were born and I have been with the family ever since.'

'Was he a handful?'

Cecile smiled reminiscently.

'Alain is the eldest of three boys and a girl. He was always the most wilful and unconventional, but always the one with the charm!'

'What do his brothers and sister do?'

'The youngest is Jean. He is in Paris training to be a doctor. Alain's sister, Marie-Claire is a lawyer like their father, and Henri, he is a fireman. I must show you the family album, if you would like.'

'Very much.'

'They are all good children, but Alain, he is my special boy.'

'You must have missed him when he went away.'

'But of course. When he left home to travel the world with his tennis, it was like losing a part of me.'

'I've never followed sport so I don't remember him from then, only the stories,' Annabel admitted. 'He hasn't told me about that time.'

'I heard the things they said about him. Half of me thinks, no, my Alain is not like this.'

'And the other half?' Annabel prompted, intrigued to learn more about him even as she was trying to distance her feelings to make leaving easier.

Cecile picked up another fork and sighed.

'There was always a rebelliousness in Alain, even as a young boy. I do not know why when he had everything, the love of his family most of all. Perhaps he had to work that side of him from his system, who can say?

'Of course, there is still something of the rogue about him, no? But he is a kind and generous man. He works hard and gives much of his time. Who can deny him his moments of play?'

Annabel studied Cecile's face, vaguely disturbed that her own instinct appeared correct and there was a side of Alain that still remained very much untamed. Perhaps the bad boy was not so reformed after all.

'Alain has a busy social life,' Cecile continued, rising to her feet and crossing the kitchen to pour two cups of coffee. She set them on the table, sat down again, and smiled. 'But he rarely has house guests, so it is a treat for me to have you around the place.'

'It is a treat for me to be in such a warm and welcoming home,' Annabel smiled back.

'Alain's girlfriends ... ' Cecile paused a moment, and an uncomfortable tension caused Annabel's chest to constrict. 'His friendships with women have been ... how do you say? Not serious, yes?

'I think his life before, in tennis, has made him cautious of his affections. I mean, he is more careful about giving of himself. And with Yvette — '

Annabel started at Cecile's words, the way the sentence was abruptly snapped off and the disconcerted expression in the Frenchwoman's eyes.

'Yvette? I have heard her mentioned before,' Annabel allowed, hoping all emotion was hidden from her voice as she gave Cecile the opening.

In the strained silence that followed, Annabel wished she had not given in to her curiosity. She felt awkward because it was not her place to ask about Alain's private life. He would not thank her for going behind his back to Cecile, and yet she had been intrigued, concerned, about Yvette and her place in Alain's life.

Cecile cleared her throat, her gazed averted.

'I do not think Alain would wish me to speak of her, Annabel. I am sorry, I should not have talked as I did. Please, forget that I said this.'

'Of course.'

As they worked for some moments in silence, Annabel reflected on what had happened. Her doubts about Alain and Yvette remained. If she was nothing in his life, why were there so many veiled references?

She bit her lip, reaffirming her resolutions of the previous night, to guard her feelings with more care until she could leave. Alain Ducret was too dangerous and too much for her to think about.

'Now I have my Alain back,' Cecile said, the heavily-accented voice drawing Annabel from her reverie. 'When my husband died some years ago, suddenly I was alone, not really needed any more at Alain's family home in Grenoble. So, Alain brought me to this villa.'

'You clearly care about him a great deal.'

'I love him as if he were my own son. He has been a blessing to my long life,' Cecile admitted with a feeling and sincerity that touched Annabel's heart. 'It is nice to have him so much about the villa.

'I have you to thank for that, ma

chére. Usually he is dashing here and there at all hours. Sometimes I am lonely when he is away on his business with the charity . . . '

As Cecile spread her hands in a typically Gallic gesture, her words trailing off, Annabel raised an interested eyebrow.

'The charity?'

'He has not told you of his work?'

'No. But then I am only here for a day or two thanks to his kindness when I was in trouble.'

'You must ask him, ma chére. He is proud of what has been achieved, but he does not . . . Oh! What is that expression you English have?' Cecile asked with a frustrated laugh. 'You know, he is modest. You say . . . ?'

'He doesn't like to blow his own trumpet?' Annabel suggested with an amused grin, unable to imagine Alain being so vulnerable and reticent.

'This is it exactly!' Cecile laughed with delight. 'I shall remember now, thank you. But I am an old woman who talks too much! Tell me more about yourself, ma chére. You have a family also, yes?'

As they continued to work through the canteen of cutlery which Annabel discovered was an heirloom of Cecile's, she spoke about her parents, her siblings, told her about the bookshop, and about Robbie.

Before she knew where she was, the morning had raced by. Cecile had been so easy to talk to, and she had opened up about herself far more than she usually would, Annabel realised with surprise. They shared a salad for lunch, and then Annabel went out to explore and to visit the bank.

Armed with directions from Cecile, she walked along the Boulevard d'Italie and into the Boulevard des Moulins, and found the bank without too much trouble. Her business completed with courtesy and efficiency, a wad of francs and travellers' cheques in her possession, Annabel stepped back outside and considered her options.

She discovered that the bus routes were interlocking and allowed access to all points of the Principality. She purchased a multiple-journey ticket, stamped it in the machine provided inside the bus, and soon found herself in the Place d'Armes at the base of the Rock of Monaco.

She explored some of the shops around the district of La Condamine backing the harbour, buying a new bag to accommodate her new belongings, some basic toiletries to supplement those provided in the bathroom at the villa.

To her delight, she discovered a bookshop that catered for the English where she chatted for a few moments with the owner and browsed happily amongst the shelves. Afterwards, she bought a few postcards and retired to a café for a drink and to write her greetings home.

She lingered at her table, enjoying the caress of the sun on her skin and admiring the view over the harbour. The

Mediterranean shimmered a spectacular blue-green in the light, silver streaks marking the crests of the ripples. She did not think she had ever been in a more perfect place.

Although she had intended to spend the time planning her immediate future, it was with resignation and a certain inevitability that she admitted Alain still dominated her thoughts.

Cecile had been open and informative, providing an insight to Alain and details Annabel had not known. His family situation was similar to her own. She, too, was the eldest of four. Her two younger brothers, Adam and David, were both at university, and Karen, her little sister, was still at school.

She had enjoyed listening to Cecile fill in the gaps about Alain, and wondered once more what his business was, this charity that occupied so much of his time and energy and took him away to other countries.

Against her better judgement, she

found herself dwelling on the information about Alain's girlfriends. There was no justification for the rush of something that was almost akin to jealousy that smarted inside her, she admonished herself.

How many times did she have to tell herself that she must ignore any attraction to Alain Ducret? Even if Yvette was not a part of his life, if he had no current female, she had been warned he was not the kind of man to be serious . . . was certainly not the kind of man for her.

Irritated with herself, she wandered back along the boulevard. After posting her cards, she discovered the picturesque church of Ste Devote. Set back in the protective bowl of rock, it was a delightful building, and she resolved to ask Cecile or Alain about it before she left.

She walked up the hill, enjoying the view of the harbour, until she reached the square that boasted the splendid Hotel de Paris and the famous façade of the casino. Annabel was about to turn to walk along the terrace, when she hesitated. Surely that was Alain's Ferrari? The car pulled up outside the hotel, and she watched as Alain opened the driver's door and stepped out.

She was about to hail him, when the passenger door opened and a redhead joined Alain. They appeared to be arguing. The red-head — was this Yvette? — shrugged free of Alain's hold and preceded him into the hotel.

Annabel's shoulders slumped as she turned away, and her walk back to the villa passed almost unnoticed as she was lost in thought once more.

It was late afternoon when she entered the villa, and there was no sign of Alain. Cecile was busy with dinner and declined her offer of assistance, so Annabel took her purchases upstairs, then went to the library with her book to curl up on the comfortable, leather sofa.

She must have dozed off, as the sound of the door closing startled her.

For a moment she could not think where she was, then as her eyes flickered open, she encountered Alain's dark brown gaze as he leaned over her, an indulgent smile curving his mouth.

Dressed in faded jeans and a sweatshirt, his hair damp from the shower, a shadow of stubble darkened his jaw and added to his rakish air. As her pulse began to race at the sight of him, Annabel knew that despite all her protestations to the contrary, she was in trouble.

'You look lovely, chérie.' He smiled, giving her a brief but effective kiss before stepping away. 'Dinner is ready.'

'How long have you been back?' Annabel asked as she took a steadying breath and swung her legs to the floor.

'Only a short while, ma chére. I came from Italy with only enough time to shower before dinner.'

Annabel remained silent as she followed Alain. He had lied, but why? What had he to hide about his meeting with the red-head? Discomforted, she fought to regain her composure and took her place at the table.

'You have had a successful day, I hope, Annabel,' Alain commented as they began their meal.

'Yes, thank you. And you?' she asked politely, hoping nothing in her voice would give her away.

'Most satisfactory.' He smiled at Cecile, then those dark eyes, the colour of molasses, refocused on her once more. 'And has Cecile been filling your head with my past misdemeanours while I have been gone?'

'Which misdemeanours in particular?'

For a second, she wondered if he had sensed something in her manner, a sharpness she had not intended, and then he laughed, a rich and throaty sound as appreciation gleamed in his eyes.

'I am not falling for that! The less you hear of my past bad behaviour the better, I think.'

It was on the tip of her tongue to mention Yvette, but Annabel bit back the words. Alain owed her no explanations, and she did not want to embarrass Cecile, especially as the kindly woman had asked her not to mention her disclosures that morning.

'You will join me for a drink?' Alain asked after dinner.

'Thank you. A dry Martini, please.' She watched him prepare the drinks, searching for a safe topic of conversation. Then she remembered the church she had seen earlier. 'Alain, what is the story of Ste Devote?'

'She was a Corsican girl, martyred for her faith. Her body was cast adrift in a boat which was guided into the harbour of Monaco by a dove in January 303AD. Each year, her feast day is commemorated by the burning of a boat, a procession, and the blessing of the water in the harbour.' He smiled at her sad expression. 'All through history there has been such persecution of one kind or another. Ste Devote is patron here in Monaco.'

A short while later, tense, aware

Alain's gaze rested on her, Annabel turned to him and broached her planned departure.

'Alain, I am really grateful for your hospitality and your kindness,' she began, her gaze sliding from the intensity of his. 'Now that I am solvent again, I think it is time that I moved on.'

'You are unhappy in my home?'

Alain's tone matched his wounded expression, and Annabel was concerned she had offended him. The problem was she was too happy and comfortable, and being near him was far too disturbing.

'It isn't a question of being unhappy,' she began, still avoiding his gaze. 'The time has come for me to go home.'

'But your holiday is not finished, and I had such plans for the week. My diary is now clear until Friday. You will deny our time together?'

Annabel closed her mind to the disappointment of what she would be giving up and injected a firmness to her voice she was far from feeling.

'I can't impose on you any longer.'

'What nonsense is this? How could you be imposing when Cecile and I are delighted to have you with us as our honoured guest?'

'But — '

'No, Annabel.' Alain's hand captured hers, his thumb tracing a disturbing circle on the inside of her wrist. 'Tomorrow we will take a picnic into the mountains, and we will hear no more of this talk of you leaving.'

8

Replete after her share of the substantial picnic packed by Cecile, Annabel lay on her back in the fragrant grass and gazed at the mountain peaks that jutted into the clear, blue sky.

The sounds of birds and insects carried on the breeze which rustled the leaves of the trees, lush and green, in the adjacent wood. In the quiet, she could hear the stream that bubbled over rocks nearby. Straight from the mountains, the water was crystal clear and icy cold.

She knew, because deceived by the warmth of the weather, she had followed Alain's straight-faced suggestion and had a paddle. He had held her trainers, watched as she rolled up the legs of her jeans, and laughed at her shriek as she stepped in and the cold had rendered her motionless.

She had only forgiven him after he

had rescued her and gallantly rubbed warmth back into her frozen flesh, restoring the circulation.

Annabel rolled on to her stomach, propped her chin in her hands, and gazed at the man who dozed beside her. Quite how he had managed to sweep all her protests against remaining with him in Monaco aside, she still could not explain.

And yet her determination to leave had crumbled to dust in the face of his persuasive tactics. Now here she was, in a secluded alpine valley, alone with the man she had convinced herself she must resist.

'You think too much, ma chére.' The husky, accented voice carried a trace of lazy amusement. 'You are not glad you came today?'

'Of course. I have enjoyed this blissful place.'

'But not being with me?'

Annabel plucked a stem of grass and twisted it between her fingers.

'I didn't say that. You are very good to me, Alain.'

'What better way is there for a man to spend his time than with a beautiful woman?'

'Alain,' she protested, flustered by his extravagant compliment and unable to prevent the faint tide of colour that washed her face.

He turned on his side, closing the distance between them, and trailed the back of his hand down her cheek.

'It is endearing that you blush so. Has no-one told you this truth before? You doubt you are beautiful, Annabel?'

'I know I'm not,' she stated with simple honesty, thinking of all the women with whom his name had been linked at one time or another.

'Your hair shines like golden silk in the sunshine, your eyes are the clear blue of a tropical sea ... and your skin, it is so soft, so flawless,' he added, turning his hand so his fingers could trace a path over her jaw and down her throat. His voice was as caressing as his touch, and she felt her whole body grow warm and tingly. One finger moved to press softly against her cheek.

'You have a tiny dimple here when you smile.' The finger moved on to follow the outline of her lips, his voice whisper-soft as his head moved towards hers. 'And your mouth is so sweet, so kissable.'

Annabel could not move. For several seconds she thought her heart had ceased to beat, then as his lips brushed hers, it resumed at a frantic pace. Her resistance crumbled. But as she leaned towards him, Alain pulled away.

Her eyes fluttered open in confusion and met his smoky gaze. They stared at each other for a moment and then he smiled and rolled on to his back. Annabel drew in a shaky breath both puzzled and sorry at his withdrawal, and yet grateful for the reprieve.

In the quiet moments that followed, Annabel tried not to dwell on what had happened between them, on Alain's words, on his skilful manipulation of her will. She lowered her head to rest it on her folded arms, her face turned away from him.

The morning had been carefree, and there was no denying Alain was fun to be with. It was true she was glad not to have missed this beautiful scenery, and there was so much more she was eager to explore in Monaco which would be more rewarding shared with him. She looked back at him relaxing beside her, his hands linked behind his head.

Perhaps she should grasp this opportunity and allow herself to be happy, to enjoy this interlude before she returned to her ordinary life in England. Could a few more days really hurt?

However much she told herself to leave, and however foolish she knew it was to become even this much involved with him, she did not think she was quite ready to say goodbye to Alain. He intrigued her, excited her.

'Alain?' she murmured after a few more moments of thought.

'Mmm?'

'Why did you quit tennis?'

He turned his head to look at her, the dark eyes watchful as he considered her question.

'I was tired of the circus, the travel, the notoriety. The money and the winning became too important, and no longer the enjoyment of the sport, you understand? One day I looked at myself and my shallow life, and I did not like the picture. And so I said to myself it was enough.'

Annabel thought of his home, devoid of all visible signs of his former profession.

'Do you regret it?'

'The playing, or the giving up?' he asked with a smile.

'Either. Both.' Annabel smiled back.

'It is the past — I cannot change it. There were many good times, and I am thankful for the chance, the success. The tennis, and the endorsements that went with it, have given me a more than comfortable life now, investments for a secure future, and the time and opportunity to use my name and do what I can to help others.

'But,' he added, 'I do not miss the life, nor do I want to remember it all the time. I was foolish, headstrong — the clichéd angry young man taking on the world! I did some crazy things, was caught up in a life that was not real. I am not proud of that, of what I was then. But I grew up and I moved on.'

She admired him for stepping away from the temptations of fame, yet for all his words, the feeling that he still held something back remained.

'Cecile mentioned you were involved with a charity now.'

'Yes. It is how I spend my time.'

Annabel sat up to face him.

'Tell me about it.'

'It is a small foundation that we run to aid children. All kinds of children in all kinds of places with all kinds of needs. We help them any way we can, with clothes, food, medicines, opportunities to do things and see things that the rest of us take for granted every day of our lives.'

Touched by his sincere words and his humility, her respect and admiration for him increased. Alain Ducret was a very special man. Without conscious thought, she reached out and rested her hand against his face, the roughness of his stubbled jaw pleasing against her skin.

'No wonder Cecile is so proud of you.'

Alain covered her hand with his, his eyes closing as he turned his head and pressed a kiss to her palm.

'Cecile is biased — and she always sees the good in people.'

'Perhaps there is a lot of good to see.' Annabel withdrew her hand from his and knotted her fingers in her lap. 'She loves you very much, Alain.'

'And I her. She has been an important anchor in my life.'

'You rescued her from loneliness.'

Alain reached out to tuck some flyaway strands of hair behind her ear.

'I just wanted her to know she was needed, that she had a place and a purpose. That is all.'

Annabel felt so close to him at that moment, loving his sensitivity, his kindness and understanding. She had come to learn so much about this complex man, things she doubted he was accustomed to sharing freely. She could only wonder that he had spoken with such candour to her, a near stranger.

The pull of his attraction increased, making it harder for her to keep a check on her emotions, and making her begin to doubt her own doubts about him and the unknown Yvette.

Tuesday drew to a close, and moved too quickly through Wednesday into Thursday. Annabel remained captivated by Monaco — and by Alain.

Together they had explored more of the Principality, including memorable visits to the Exotic Gardens with its interesting plants, steep pathways and incredible views, and also the deep and beautiful grottos, all two hundred and fifty steps down and back up again!

Yesterday had brought news from Inspector Bonneau that her car had been found by the police at an isolated spot near Lyon. Alain had told her the worst — that only the shell was left, burned out and abandoned. Everything had gone. It was stupid to be sentimental about an inanimate object, Annabel knew, but she felt great sadness at the loss of her car.

She and Robbie had bought it together after she had passed her driving test, and it held many happy memories.

Alain was sympathetic in response to her moment of distress. To help her take her mind off the bad news, they had gone out after another of Cecile's marvellous meals to a nightclub where they had danced for hours.

Held in his arms, with his lips brushing her skin, and the sound of his whispered words in French, she had forgotten everything but being with him, her whole being fired with a prickling excitement.

In contrary fashion, she had begun to wish that Alain would not keep so rigidly to his promise, and would offer her more than the briefest tantalising good-night kiss.

Now it was late afternoon on Thursday, and the clock was ticking on towards the end of her holiday. She had vowed to make the most of every moment, wanting to build a catalogue of memories to take home with her to England, memories of Alain and Monaco and an unforgettable experience.

Tomorrow, Alain was scheduled to take another trip for the foundation that would take him away for the whole day. It signified an end to their time together as she would have to return home after the weekend. But this evening, Alain had promised her a surprise.

She stood at the picture window in the living-room and looked out at the swimming pool where Alain stroked effortlessly back and forth. He swam with grace and skill, characteristics that carried through into every aspect of his life. She enjoyed looking at him. His body was tanned, athletic, muscles rippling under supple skin. How was she ever going to leave him?

In the past days she had discovered so much about him; important things such as his compassion, his humour; little things like his favourite foods, his passion for sports, especially ski-ing, his weakness for fast cars. And he had drawn her out about herself, stories of her past, her family, her old dreams that had died with Robbie.

What she did not share with him was the birth of new dreams . . . dreams in which she tried to convince herself Alain played no part.

She felt she had known him for ever. Was it really only a week since he had rescued her from the roadside? In that short time, her emotions had become involved in a way she had never expected, nor wanted them to be.

However familiar to her, Alain was a recent acquaintance. She was no closer now than she had ever been to discovering if there was someone in his life, if the mysterious Yvette was part of the past or the present.

While her doubts remained unsolved, however blurred, she had to be cautious. Alain's playboy past still caused her concern. It was a lifestyle with which she was unfamiliar, and wary of being hurt she would do well to guard her heart until she was sure.

'Annabel?'

Startled from her reverie, she turned and stepped away from the window, hoping her observation of Alain had escaped Cecile's attention.

'I have remembered the photographs for you to see, ma chére.'

She smiled, crossing to sit on the sofa and patting the cushion beside her. Annabel joined her, and soon she was lost in the story of Alain's life that unfolded for her. Alain as a baby, a schoolboy, a lanky teenager, a long-haired troublemaker on the tennis courts.

124

'Cecile, not the family photographs!' Alain rebuked with mock sternness.

Annabel glanced up from the pages. Framed in the doorway with a towel looped round his neck, his only clothing was a pair of black swim shorts. His golden skin glistened with droplets of water, and his dark hair was slicked back from his face. He looked wonderful.

'You were very smart in your school uniform on your first day at school,' Annabel teased to cover her heated reaction to the sight of him.

'Cecile, how could you do this to me?' Alain rolled his eyes in despair.

'I am showing Annabel how nice you were when you were young.'

Cecile's snappy rejoinder made Alain laugh, and there was a light in his eyes when his gaze turned back to Annabel.

'I am going upstairs to dress. I will see you soon.'

'When are you going to tell me where you are taking me tonight?'

'All in good time.'

'Then how will I know what to wear?'

His hands loosely held the ends of his towel as he regarded her for a long moment, then a smile curved his mouth.

'Come with me. I have something for you.'

Intrigued, Annabel thanked Cecile and excused herself, then followed Alain upstairs. She hovered in the doorway of his bedroom as he tossed his towel on a chair then picked up a large box from the top of a chest of drawers. He carried it across to her and held it as she took off the lid and fumbled through layers of fine tissue paper.

'Alain,' she breathed in wonderment, as she uncovered an exquisite designer dress in slim-fitting beaded emerald. 'I can't accept this.'

'Annabel, do not start that again.'

'But — '

'Chérie, Chantal and I picked this out especially for you. Will you not at least wear it this evening?' he cajoled. 'You will look so beautiful.'

'You really want me to?' Eyes wide, she gazed up at him.

'I hardly intended to wear it myself!'

Annabel laughed at the absurdity of his teasing and accepted the box without further argument.

'Thank you.'

'I shall meet you in the library at seven thirty.'

'Where — '

'No!' he forestalled with a shake of his head. 'I will not divulge my plans for the evening! Don't keep me waiting.'

★   ★   ★

Annabel sat opposite Alain at their table in the ornate Imperial Room at the Hotel de Paris and hoped she did not look as awestruck as she felt.

Her first impressions of the famous luxury hotel, from its attractive, ornamental façade to the sumptuous interior, had still not worn off. Nor had a renewed flicker of doubt.

Was it by chance or design that Alain had brought her to the very place she had seen him with the red-head last Monday? The question remained at the back of her mind.

Alain, an attractive and witty escort, still had the smile of amusement in his dark eyes at her reaction to her surroundings and her recognition of several famous celebrities with whom they shared the dining hall.

And as for the food, the meal was a triumph of French gastronomic artistry which she knew she would never forget and doubted she would taste the like of again.

Annabel reached out for her glass and took a sip of wine, glancing at Alain from beneath her lashes. Dressed in a white dinner jacket and black trousers, his white silk shirt offset by a black bow tie, he looked heartstopping ... handsome and sophisticated, and still not entirely tamed. Meeting his sultry brown gaze, she smiled.

'I feel like Cinderella,' she murmured, inhibited by the glamour, the elegant women with their expensive air and even more expensive jewels.

Alain reached out to take her hand, his fingers linking with hers.

'Believe me, ma chére, you need no adornment to enhance your beauty. You are the most stunning woman here. And that dress is a triumph!'

Annabel had to admit that Chantal's creation had surpassed her wildest imaginings. The beaded fabric shimmered and danced in the light, and moulded her body like a second skin, accentuating every curve. Tiny straps fanned out from the front of the choker neck to support the bodice.

The open back dipped to her waist, and a deep slit ran up one side from the hem to mid-thigh. Chantal had even provided matching evening shoes and bag.

She wore no jewellery, and a touch of warm lipstick was the only makeup she had used. Her skin had a healthy glow, and her eyes were clear and long-lashed, their colour highlighted by the fire of the dress.

Alain's gaze had all but devoured her when she had joined him in the library of the villa on the dot of seven thirty. The warmth and edge of dangerous excitement that had sparked within her at his reaction and appraisal still smouldered.

She was about to thank him again when she heard his swift, indrawn breath, and she glanced at him in surprise. His expression had tightened and a flicker of alarm danced in her stomach.

'Alain? What is it?'

He was gazing past her towards the entrance to the Imperial Room, and for several moments, he appeared not to have heard her. Then, as she was about to turn round to see what had arrested his attention and caused his tension, he refocused that disturbing gaze on her.

'Nothing that need concern you,' he

murmured in response, his gaze flicking away once more before he smiled back at her, a smile that did not banish the shadows from his eyes. 'I think it is time for us to move on.'

Before she could comment, Alain was by her side, waiting for her to rise. As she complied, his hand rested against the small of her back, and he guided her towards the twin figures that marked the doorway beneath the decorative fresco. Bemused by his behaviour, Annabel took a surreptitious glance around the dining hall.

On the far side of the room she saw a willowy red-head arrive at a table. It was the same woman she had seen with Alain before, and she was watching them leave. Even from this distance Annabel felt the chill of her hostile stare.

Disconcerted, she halted beside Alain in the foyer beside a large bronze statue of Louis XIV astride a horse. She glanced at Alain but could now find no trace of his discomfort.

Had she imagined it? Was her mind playing tricks on her, her doubts making her see things, think things, that had no relevance? Or had Alain brought her here deliberately? Was that why he had wanted her to wear the dress?

9

There has not been time for you to enjoy the rich cultural life that Monaco has to offer, chérie, but no visit would be complete without once visiting the casino.' Alain smiled, for all the world as if nothing had happened. 'See how one leg of the horse statue is shiny? It is superstition, but rub it for luck.'

Attempting to set her concerns aside, unwilling yet to question Alain further, Annabel smiled and did as she was told. As they left the hotel and walked across the road, she took a breath of the evening air.

This place had a special magic. Lighting enhanced the façade of the casino and the trees and formal gardens that were laid out across the square from the entrance.

They entered the building and Annabel smiled as they moved to the left towards the gaming rooms. Alain organised their admittance, and although he did not visit the casino often, he was known, and she was accepted as his guest without the need of her passport.

While Alain bought a stack of chips, Annabel gazed round the busy salons, awed once more by the grandeur, the size and opulence . . . all the gilding, paintings, the glittering chandeliers, the cheeky nymphs on a ceiling. It was magnificent, baroque, and faintly decadent. Annabel loved it.

For a while they toured the gaming tables, enjoying a few wins and commiserating with fellow patrons over losses. Annabel had never gambled before, and she was staggered by the sums involved and by the casual attitude of many of the people to the winning and losing of money.

Alain made a couple of small and unsuccessful wagers on cards and dice, and then they moved on. When space became available at a roulette table,

Alain held out a chair for her and she sat down, gasping when he put a stack of chips into her hands.

'Alain — '

'Pick a number, Annabel.'

How much the chips represented, Annabel dared not ask.

'I can't,' she whispered, gazing up at him appealingly.

'You only bet what you can afford to lose,' he assured her, his voice husky as he stooped to murmur against her ear.

'But — ' Annabel was not reassured.

'Place the bet. It is only for fun, yes?'

Fun? She was terrified to have the fate of Alain's money resting in her hands. The palms of her hands felt clammy, and her heart began to thunder in her chest.

'Go on. Be brave,' Alain urged with a soft laugh.

Her fingers shaking, adrenalin pumping in her veins, Annabel slowly slid the chips to the number twenty-seven. As the wheel was spun, she almost snatched them all back again. Alain stood behind her and rested a hand on her bare shoulders, his touch warm, his fingers caressing.

The ball was rolled. Annabel couldn't look. Gripping Alain's other hand in both of hers, she peeked between her lashes in fascinated dread, watching with bated breath as the wheel began to slow. Her body began to tremble with fear and tension. If she lost all that money she would never forgive herself, but the odds of her winning had to be astronomical.

The ball bobbed and bounced, teasing and tantalising as it skipped from number to number. To Annabel, it seemed time passed in slow motion before the wheel halted. She heard Alain laugh, then she stared in amazement at the sight of the ball resting in the number twenty-seven slot.

They had won! She hadn't lost Alain's money! The thrill of victory seized her, and she laughed up at Alain as the winnings to piled up in front of her.

'I don't believe it!'

'You have the Midas touch.' Alain congratulated her, his fingers still tracing their disturbing path on her skin. 'Are you going to ride your luck?'

'Definitely not! I shall quit while I'm ahead. I couldn't stand that tension a second time.'

'Still playing it safe, chérie?'

Annabel's gaze locked with his as she read the hidden meaning in his soft challenge. If he was asking her how much more time she needed to make up her mind about a relationship with him, she could not answer. Instead, she returned her attention to the table and began to gather up the enormous pile of chips, pushing them towards Alain.

'No, ma chére. You won it, you keep it.'

'I can't do that,' she protested in a shocked whisper.

She stood up, breaking the contact of his fingers on her tingling flesh, and with determination, she began putting the chips into the pockets of Alain's jacket. He regarded her with amused exasperation.

'We make a deal,' he suggested. 'I put up the stake, but you choose the number. So, we shall split the winnings in half, yes?'

Annabel chewed her bottom lip in silent consideration, unable to feel comfortable about the amount of money he insisted she should have.

'All right,' she finally conceded with reluctance.

'Now that is settled, we shall adjourn for a celebration.'

Alain slid an arm around her waist and led her from the salon. He ordered champagne, and sat down close to her — very close.

Annabel sipped her champagne, feeling distinctly light-headed after the wine at dinner and the potent effect of Alain's nearness. She glanced at him and found him watching her, the dark eyes hot with unhidden desire.

A movement near the bar distracted her attention, and she was momentarily relieved to drag her gaze from the intensity of his. The feeling was short-lived. With a shock, she met the angry, cold gaze of the red-head who sat on a high stool at the counter.

Annabel froze. Was it coincidence that everywhere Alain took her the other woman appeared as well? Unable to help her reaction, she recoiled from Alain.

'Chérie?' He frowned and followed the direction of her gaze. 'Mon dieu, Yvette!'

Annabel looked at him from beneath her lashes, surprised to see his customary equanimity so rattled.

'Alain, just who is Yvette? I've heard her mentioned. Every time I turn around, there she is.'

'Forget it, Annabel. It is of no importance.'

'Alain — '

'I do not wish to discuss it,' he interrupted, his expression closed, his jaw tense with annoyance. 'We will leave.'

Without another word, Alain took the glass from her hand, set it on the table, and drew her to her feet. Tension hummed between them as they left the casino and made the short journey back to the villa. Nerves knotted inside her as she stepped into the marbled hall and Alain closed the door.

The house was quiet and still. Annabel remembered that Cecile had gone to spend the night with old friends in Menton, a twice-monthly occurrence and she was not due back until lunchtime the next day.

This meant that she and Alain were alone. Nervous, she walked into the living-room, aware that Alain followed her. She stood at the window looking out at the Principality aglow.

'Would you like some more champagne?' Alain asked from behind her.

Annabel could see his reflection in the glass as he raised his hands to her shoulders.

'Chérie?'

'No. No more champagne, thank you.'

Was that her voice, all trembly and throaty? His fingers brushed the short strands of hair aside, and she started when she felt his lips trail along the back of her neck. How could she ignore what had happened that evening? She shouldn't let him do this, had to stop him.

'Alain . . . '

He turned her round and cupped her face in his hands. He had not switched on the lights, and shadows cloaked his features as he looked down at her.

Then he silenced her half-formed protests with an earth-shattering kiss.

All thought, all doubt, ceased. She had no awareness of moving into his arms. She just clung to him, her fingers sinking into the thickness of his hair as he wrapped one arm around her hips and drew her to him, the fingers of the other hand whispering over the bare skin of her back.

Annabel shivered as his lips left hers to glide a path of sweet heat down her throat. His touch was like wildfire, teasing all her senses to life, overwhelming her, and the husky timbre of his voice as he whispered to her almost made her melt.

'You know how I feel about you.'

His breath fanned her neck as his lips brushed to her ear.

'Do you want me to tell you?'

'I know.' She struggled through a whirl of sensation.

He was weaving a sensual web around her. She was so tempted to give up the fight, but sufficient doubts persisted to make her hold back.

'But you are not ready, are you, my dearest? Not just yet,' he supplied for her, his lips grazing back across her cheek to capture her mouth once more and steal her answer.

Annabel sighed as he pulled back from her a scant millimetre.

'I can't, Alain.' There was so much she still had to know about him, things he had shown this evening he would not talk about.

'How long are you going to mourn him?'

Despite his whispered question, Annabel knew that Robbie was no longer the issue between them, the reason why she hesitated. However heady and passionate it would be, she was not sure she could handle a brief relationship with Alain — even if she was sure he were free.

But Yvette remained between them, mysterious, unmentioned, but a threat just the same. Until she was sure in her own mind . . . The thoughts trailed off. Even then, she knew that an affair would belittle how she had come to feel for Alain in this short time — feelings she had still not dared admit to herself.

Alain was a renowned playboy, although he had made strenuous efforts to convince her he had changed. Was he really so different? Could she trust her feelings? It had all happened so fast, her senses scattered before the whirlwind of

Alain's attention.

Alain held her for a moment longer, resting his chin on the top of her head. She breathed in the scent of him. If only she could resolve her confusion. It felt so good to be with him, but how could she ignore the fact that she must leave in another couple of days? How could she ignore Yvette? When Alain stepped away from her, she felt bereft.

'You had better go to bed,' he advised, an edge of mockery in his tone, his eyes unreadable as he looked at her. 'I don't think you want to discuss this any longer.'

With the approach of dawn, Annabel heard Alain leave the villa for his business trip. Or was it a business trip? Was he going to meet Yvette as he had last Monday? She wished she could be sure.

For now she would be left with no answers to her many questions. Alain expected to be back late, and she would not see him until sometime on Saturday. Then only Sunday would be left of her stay in Monaco. Today she had to contact the consulate again to arrange a travel document for Monday. She would catch the train to Marseille and fly back to Gatwick from there.

Home. Away from Alain.

After Sunday, there would be no more time with him — no more kisses, no more opportunities. The prospect made her unutterably sad. With hindsight, it was easy to say she should never have allowed him to persuade her to stay. But she had stayed. She had wanted the taste of paradise and now she would have to pay the price.

The house felt empty when she rose and dressed shortly after Alain's departure. She felt lonely without him, her heart heavy with the weight of her confusion. It was a beautiful morning, still and clear, and she let herself out of the villa for an early walk to blow the cobwebs from her mind.

She passed the Carmelite church and took the route Alain had shown her down the stone steps and through the tunnel that emerged near the Beach Plaza Hotel. She crossed the road and walked a short distance along the promenade before she went down on to the public beach.

From a distance this beach had looked sandy, but Annabel discovered it was man-made from countless millions of tiny white stones. She picked up a handful, letting them trickle through her fingers, and on a whim, she slipped a few into the pocket of her denim shorts for a souvenir.

Taking off her shoes, she found that the beach was not at all uncomfortable as she stepped down to the shore. The sea was warm, lapping gently round her ankles . . . not at all like the mountain stream. A smile curved her mouth as she recalled the trick Alain had played on her.

Just thinking about him made her warm, but there was a deep sadness that her time with him was almost over. So why did she waste a moment of it worrying and thinking? Hadn't her shattering experience over the loss of Robbie taught her to make the most of time, of happiness?

The Principality began to stir as the sun rose higher in the blue sky. A decision had been made. She would talk to Alain, clear the air of misunderstandings, make the most of the time left. Filled with a building of nervous excitement, Annabel walked back to the villa for breakfast.

When she saw the front door was ajar, she hesitated, a frown of concern on her face. She had closed it, she was certain. Maybe Cecile was back early — or Alain? Annabel stepped inside and halted at the sight of a set of designer luggage stacked on the marble floor.

Before she could formulate a single thought, a noise drew her gaze upwards. Yvette, tall and willowy, walked along the gallery from the direction of Alain's bedroom. She descended the stairs with sinuous grace.

On the surface she was beautiful,

elegant and poised in a way that spoke of money and style. But as she approached and Annabel saw her for the first time close to, she discovered that Yvette had the coldest, hardest eyes she had ever seen. Ice-blue, they showed not a spark of humanity.

Annabel forced down a rising tide of dread as Yvette stared at her, her face a mask of mocking dislike.

'What are you doing here?' she managed, her voice more unsteady than she had wished.

'I live here.' She rested her manicured hands on narrow hips, her mouth twisted in a sneer. 'You think that you, Annabel, the little English waif Alain picked up on the road to amuse him, can take my place?'

10

Annabel leaned back against the front door for support, feeling sick inside as Yvette stared at her with icy hostility and the poisonous assault continued.

'Alain is using you to get back at me. We had a lovers' tiff. It has happened before. He wants me back and is trying to make me jealous.' Yvette's thickly-accented voice paused as she cast a derisive glance over her. 'You do not think he was ever interested in you, do you? I have heard all about you. Alain likes to have his bet, how long it will take him to seduce you while he waits for me to come home.'

'I don't believe you,' Annabel whispered as pain tightened inside her.

'Why do you think he introduces you to our friends, knowing word will reach me? Why do you think he brings you to places where I am?' A hint of malice appeared on Yvette's face as each cruel dart hit home. 'You think Alain does not laugh at you? You think that you could possibly be anything but a game to a man such as Alain?'

Stunned and speechless with the shock and hurt inflicted by Yvette and her revelations, Annabel felt her body begin to tremble. Still Yvette went on without remorse.

'I know all about Alain's dalliances with women. Again and again I forgive him. Now I do this again. He has persuaded me to move back in. We are meant to be together. You have served your purpose, English girl, but it is me he wants in his life. I am back. Alain is bored with you. Go home.'

Tears stung Annabel's eyes, but she refused to give the other woman the satisfaction of seeing them and the evidence of how deeply she had wounded her. With as much calm and dignity as she could muster, Annabel walked past Yvette without a word and went upstairs to the room that had been hers for the last week.

She had to put as much distance between herself and this place before Alain returned tonight. In a daze of shock and pain, she packed her meagre belongings in her bag.

All the clothes Alain had bought for her with the exception of the T-shirt she was wearing with her shorts, she left hanging in the wardrobe, the beaded emerald dress packed back in its box in protective tissue paper.

Two tears escaped and rolled down her cheeks. She dashed them away with the back of her hand. Alain was not worth crying over. How could he do this? She could not afford to think about him and his duplicity or she would fall apart.

There was no sign of Yvette when she left the room for the last time and walked round the gallery to Alain's office. It was only when she sat at his desk that she saw the photograph tucked in a position that meant it would have been hidden from her view the last time she had been in this room.

It was in a silver frame, a colour portrait of Alain and Yvette that appeared to have been taken on the same occasion as the one in the cutting she had seen at Chantal's boutique.

All the painful things Yvette had said had to be true. If Alain had this picture on his desk . . . With unsteady fingers, Annabel picked up a pen. The note she wrote him was brief but polite, and it contained none of the bitter anger that raged inside her.

She folded the paper into an envelope and enclosed the money he had given her, the winnings from the casino. She wanted nothing from him, would not let herself feel she had been bought.

After writing a warmer note of thanks and regret for her rapid departure to Cecile which she propped on the dressing table in the housekeeper's rooms, Annabel walked down the stairs, her head held high.

She closed the front door behind her,

thankful to have escaped without another encounter with Yvette. As she walked down the road, she refused to look back.

It was only after she had reached the railway station, telephoned the consulate to make an appointment and was aboard the train that whisked her away to Marseille, that reaction overtook her. The tears she had battled to hold in check now poured down her cheeks in an unstoppable torrent.

She had not thought she could ever hurt like this again, not after Robbie. But the knowledge that Alain had been playing a cruel game with her, amusing himself as he used her to make Yvette jealous, hurt with all the violence of a dagger being plunged repeatedly into her heart.

The fairytale had turned into a nightmare. Now, when it was far too late to protect herself, Annabel realised how completely and stupidly she had fallen in love with Alain.

He had rescued her from thieves,

only to steal her heart himself — a heart that had been broken once by Robbie's death, had awoken from a protective numbness to reach instinctively for Alain, only to be broken for a second time in the cruellest of ways.

Annabel brushed the tears from her cheeks and huddled in her seat, grateful she was alone in her part of the carriage. She had never been so humiliated. And it was little comfort to have found out about Alain's deception now before things had gone any further between them.

How stupid she had been to allow herself to believe, even for a moment, that Alain could be interested in her in any way. Those expert kisses that had set her on fire and robbed her of reason had just been a tool of the trade to a philanderer.

Heaven knew, there had been enough warnings from his past, enough doubts about Yvette, but she had allowed herself to be convinced he had changed. But while the outward appearance of the rebel may now be veneered with the gloss of respectability, the wild rake still lurked within.

She knew he had lied to her about his return from Milan when she had seen him with Yvette. She had known the shadow of Yvette almost from the first. Alain had been evasive, clandestine.

He had shown her off to his friends, made sure she was dressed up to parade in front of Yvette for his own ends. He hadn't cared at all about her feelings. She wanted no part of his kind of world.

How he and his friends must have laughed at her naïveté. She had been so blind, so convinced by his show of generosity and kindness, swept off her feet by his charm and the appeal that had played havoc with her reason.

Any inner healing that had begun on this trip had been reversed with Yvette's disclosure of Alain's treachery. Annabel could actually feel herself retreat into the numbing, protective shell that had cloaked her in the months since Robbie's death.

Every word the Frenchwoman had said still lanced inside her shattered heart. And the delight she had taken in hurting her . . . How could the Alain she had known for the past week be involved with such a cold and callous woman?

But then she had not known the real Alain, had she? Instead, she had been swept off her feet by his attention, his magnetism, and she had lost all reason and commonsense. Surely she knew by now that fairytales were just that. There were no happy endings, Cinderellas and Prince Charmings outside the story-books.

When she reached Marseille and found the consulate, there was a delay while the necessary paperwork was attended to. From there, Annabel made her way to the airport, only to endure an even longer wait for an available flight out to Gatwick.

She arrived back in England to wind and rain. After the sheltered warmth of

Monaco, her shorts and T-shirts were inadequate protection, and she shivered as she waited for a connecting train to Eastbourne.

It was late evening when she arrived home, weary and forlorn. Her brothers were away at university, her sister out at a party, so Annabel only had to present a normal front to her parents.

She gave only a sketchy outline of her holiday after the theft of the car, talking of Cecile with affection, but telling them nothing about Alain. She could not even bring herself to mention his name.

'Are you sure you're all right, darling?' her mother questioned as Annabel rose to go upstairs to her room. 'You seem ... I don't know, different, distracted.'

'I'm fine. Just tired. It's good to be home,' she added, cursing the faint wobble that crept into her voice.

Seeing more questions forming in her mother's mind, Annabel excused herself and retreated to her bedroom

— her private domain since childhood. By rights, of course, she should have had her own house with Robbie now, then she would never have known this anguish.

And but for Yvette, she would still be at the villa in a corner of paradise, waiting impatiently for Alain like a sacrificial lamb.

She squeezed her eyes shut against another wave of pain. Damn Alain. Why did she have to care so much? Why did it have to hurt like this?

She crawled into bed and pulled the blankets up to her chin. After only a week away, this room felt strange now, dark and closed after her beautiful and airy bedroom at the villa. She had to stop thinking about that, had to put Monaco and Alain behind her.

Giving in to temptation, her hand stole out and she pulled something from her bag that she had dropped by the bed. Her fingers curled into silken fabric. She tried to pretend she had packed the shirt Alain had loaned her that first night by mistake, but she knew that was a lie.

Even in her anger and her hurt, she had needed something of his to take away, something for the good memories, something against the pain. She held the silk against her face, breathing in the familiar scent of him. With a moan, she curled her body into a protective ball.

Fresh tears slid down her cheeks. Despite her anger and pain and bitterness at the way Alain had used her, her heart still yearned for the man she had thought him to be . . . the Alain she had loved.

After a night spent tossing and turning, hoping for sleep as a relief from her thoughts, and wakefulness to escape dreams filled with Alain's image, Annabel arrived downstairs too late to avoid family breakfast. She took her place at the table with reluctance and a heavy heart.

A brief glimpse in the mirror had shown her to be pale with dark circles under her dulled eyes. She had attempted to brighten herself up, but could tell from her father's paternal and doctorly concern and her mother's continual worried glances that it had not been successful.

All she could think about was Alain and his duplicity. Was he back from his trip? Had he found her note? What had he thought when he had discovered she had gone? No doubt he and Yvette had indulged in a good laugh at her expense. The thought of it brought a lash of pain.

Unable to face food, she sipped a cup of coffee and listened as her sister, Karen, always up with the lark whatever time she went to bed, gave a detailed report of her friend's party between mouthfuls of cereal. As her chatter wound down, she planted her elbows on the table and directed an impish grin at Annabel.

'Well, big sister?'

'Well what?'

'I want to hear all about Monte

Carlo, of course!' She laughed, her grey-green eyes innocent and full of fun. 'What was it like, what did you do? Did you meet anyone famous?'

'It was very beautiful and I did a lot of sightseeing.'

'Is that it?'

'Yes.'

'Humph!' she grunted with dissatisfaction. 'What about the place where you stayed? Whom did it belong to? Did you meet any gorgeous men?'

'No.' Annabel cursed the sudden snap in her voice. She blinked back a sudden and unwanted welling of tears and rose to her feet, avoiding three startled glances. With an effort, she softened the brusqueness in her voice. 'I'll tell you about it another time. If you'll excuse me, I want to go to the shop for a while.'

'But, Annabel . . . ' Her mother half rose and then sat down again.

'I'll see you later.'

She made her escape from the house, and walked to the shop via the seafront, huddled against the chill breeze off the Channel. At the western end of the town lay Beachy Head. She had been up there a time or two in the darkest days after Robbie, seeking understanding and solitude.

With a sigh, she looked out over the murky water. Even though it wasn't at its best today, whatever the attractions of the Sussex coast and the lovely surrounding countryside, it wasn't Monaco . . . and there was no Alain.

She refused to cry over him any more, she promised herself, biting her lip against the tears. It was over, she had to forget, move on to other things.

The words had a familiar ring. It was a road she had been down before. Absorbing herself in work at the bookshop, hour after hour of work, had deadened her to the pain of her loss, and she just hoped it would work a second time.

'Look at you!' Sam exclaimed in disgust when Annabel walked in the bookshop door. She was famed for her straight-talking ways, and was unable to hide her shock when she looked at Annabel.

'You were supposed to be going on a happy, relaxing holiday, not for a course of torture treatment. You look dreadful.'

'Thanks. How are things here?' Annabel gave a rueful smile.

'Fine, but you aren't supposed to be asking until Monday at the earliest. What happened?'

Annabel sat down at her desk and flicked absently through some papers.

'I had my car stolen and was robbed of all my belongings.'

'I know all that,' Sam dismissed with a wave of her hand. 'Your mum came in and told me the news. And I got your postcard from the jetset playground ... you sounded chirpy. Obviously something else happened.'

'I don't know what you're talking about.'

'Fiddlesticks. What's going on?'

Frustrated, Annabel rose to her feet and walked from the office into the main part of the bookshop.

'Nothing, Sam. I just wanted to get back to work.'

'Annabel — '

She breathed a sigh of relief when the telephone rang and Sam was forced to call a halt to her inquisition to answer it. It was obvious her friend was not convinced she was fine, any more than her family had been, but Annabel refused to say another word about Monaco or her holiday, and her lips were forever sealed on the subject of Alain.

As the morning wore on, Annabel's nerves became frayed. In between attempts to divert Sam by asking about her fiancé, her sister's new baby, and details of what had taken place in the shop while she had been away, Annabel had to endure a steady bombardment of questions.

Noon approached, and she stacked some new books on the shelves, Sam at her heels still firing questions at her one after the other, when the ping of the bell above the door announced the arrival of a customer. Grateful for the reprieve, Annabel left Sam to assist with any queries and continued with her task.

'Good grief!' Sam murmured under her breath as she walked away. 'May I help you with something, or are you just browsing?'

'Thank you, but I know what it is I have come for,' a familiar, huskily-accented voice responded.

'I see!'

In the instant before she turned round, Annabel tried to reassure herself that it could not possibly be Alain's voice, that her tortured mind was simply playing a cruel trick on her. Her agonised gaze clashed with Alain's. A flash of anger in those dark brown eyes daunted her, until she remembered that she was the one with the right to be angry, not him.

'What do you want?' she demanded, vaguely aware of Sam looking on open-mouthed.

Her gaze swept over him. He looked tired and rumpled, a day's growth of beard shadowing his jaw. Dressed in black jeans, a black shirt, and a well-worn black leather jacket, he looked dark and dangerous, and as gorgeous as ever.

His gaze released hers, and he flicked a glance at Sam.

'You are Sam, yes? I am glad to meet you,' he intoned gracefully.

'Likewise, I'm sure.'

'Now you will excuse Annabel, please,' he continued, his gaze swinging back to her. 'I am angry with her at the moment, and I think we should have our first argument in private . . . also our first making up. You understand?'

Alain's grasp on her arm was firm and overrode any resistance. As he all but dragged her from the shop, Annabel heard Sam's laughing response.

'I understand perfectly!'

11

'What do you think you are doing?' Annabel hissed as Alain guided her across the pavement and into a waiting taxi. The car drew away from the kerb, and she risked a glance at Alain's stormy face as he sat beside her. 'Where are you taking me?'

'For now we are going to your house. I have been assured by your parents of privacy.'

Annabel's eyes widened in dismay.

'You've been to my house? Spoken to my family?'

'But of course.' He slid an arm along the back of the seat. 'It seems you did not tell them the whole story of your stay in Monaco.'

Disconcerted by his nearness, Annabel shifted away from him.

'And you did?'

'I believe we now have a good

understanding,' he confirmed with maddening calm.

'How could you, Alain?'

'I do not understand why you are so upset.'

The nerve of the man! Annabel glared at him, anger keeping her nerves and her hurt at bay.

'Don't you?' she gritted with uncharacteristic sarcasm.

'It is a courtesy that I see your parents, chérie. How was I to know that you would not have explained my part in your rescue and your presence in my home?' he questioned as if it was a reasonable argument. 'I was a surprise to them.'

'I can imagine.'

The taxi drew up outside her house. Annabel swung the door open, slid out, then stalked across the pavement and up the path.

'You do things I cannot hope to fathom,' Alain complained, catching up with her at the front door. 'Why did you not tell your family about me?'

'It didn't seem important enough to mention.'

Annabel closed her mind to the pain that flashed in Alain's dark eyes at her untruthful rejoinder. It was nothing to the hurt she had suffered as a result of his lies and duplicity. Working up her anger as a means of defence, she moved into the living-room and put something solid between them before she turned to face the man she had never expected to see again.

'Well, what do you want? Why have you come here?'

'Annabel, what is the matter with you?' he asked as if perplexed. His eyes glittered with annoyance. 'Why do you think I am here?'

'I don't know, but you needn't have bothered.'

'You believe you can just run off leaving only a terse note? I came back and found you gone. Just like that,' he challenged, snapping his fingers. 'And what of Cecile? Did her kindness deserve your stealthy departure? What of the worry she experienced when you were gone from the villa?'

'I explained in my letter to Cecile,' she began defensively. 'I — '

'You explained nothing,' Alain cut in angrily.

'And I'm not going to now.'

He frowned at the stubborn set of her jaw.

'Tell me what has happened to make you this way.'

'As if you don't know.'

'But how can I know, Annabel, when you refuse to tell me?'

She gave a hollow laugh, and backed away when he stepped towards her.

'Go away and leave me alone.'

'So, you just throw the last week back in my face? You leave the clothes, the money, with your cold words, and that's it, it's over? I think not, chérie.'

She was disconcerted when he cornered her and captured her chin in his hand, forcing her to look at him, his touch branding her skin.

'Why are you doing this?' she whispered as the pain hit her. 'Enough damage has been done.'

'What are you talking about?'

'It's quite simple, Alain. I am not interested in being your temporary plaything, or someone you can have a bet and laugh over with your friends. Nor will I be used.'

Alain's expression darkened, his eyes full of anger.

'What are you saying?'

'Don't act the innocent with me,' she retorted, struggling without success to free herself from his disturbing hold. Her own anger swelled within her. 'Let me go!'

'Chérie!'

'Stop calling me that. It's a lie, like everything else was a lie. I know what you had planned, how you used me. I know the truth,' she insisted, her voice rising with the force of her turbulent emotions.

When the grip of his fingers slackened, she was able to push past him and put some distance between them. She tried to ignore the way her flesh missed his touch. She couldn't think straight when he touched her.

Why had he come here? Why make this more unpleasant and difficult? He had achieved what he wanted, his precious, callous Yvette had come home. She turned to face him once more and found him brooding.

'What are these plans you say I have, this truth of which you speak? How have I used you?' he demanded. He took a breath and softened his tone. 'Annabel, please. Remember the way we have been together.'

'I don't want to remember. I may have fallen for that Gallic charm once, but I am not stupid enough to do so a second time. I will not allow you to make a fool of me.'

Alain frowned blackly.

'Stop talking in riddles and tell me what you mean. What are you accusing me of?'

'Yvette,' she shouted, her distress

172

reflected in her voice. 'Yvette told me everything.'

'Yvette Lachaud?' Alain spat out what sounded suspiciously like a French epithet. 'Mon dieu, chérie, what has she to do with this? Tell me, what has Yvette done now?'

Annabel hesitated, uncertain at the puzzlement and weary disbelief on Alain's face.

'She's living with you. You're going to be married.'

'Hell will freeze over before that woman will be anything in my life,' he ground out with angry impatience. 'Where do you get those ideas?'

She wanted to believe him, but could she trust her feelings? Could she trust Alain? She looked at him, seething with inner doubt, and found that he watched her. He sat down in the nearest armchair and pressed the fingers of one hand to his eyes. When he spoke, his voice was full of tired confusion.

'Please, Annabel, explain this to me. I am trying to understand, but I have had no sleep since I don't know when, what with the travel, finding out you had left, worrying and chasing after you. Clearly my brain is not functioning.' He puffed out a long breath and leaned back. 'Tell me what Yvette has said and done.'

Her voice filled with pain and uncertainty, Annabel explained the events of the fateful morning. Was it really only yesterday? She told him about the open door, the luggage in the hall, Yvette's exit from his bedroom, every cruel and wounding word she had said, the photograph on his desk.

When she had finished, Alain looked thunderous. He rose to his feet and paced the floor, muttering to himself in French.

He halted in front of her, his eyes dark with anger and hurt.

'So you left? You walked away, discarded all we had been, condemned me on the word of a cold and heartless woman?'

'Alain . . . ' Annabel reeled under his unexpected attack. 'I was so hurt, so humiliated. I thought — '

'I am hurt, too, by your lack of trust in me. Despite what you have come to know of me, you took her word.'

'I'm sorry . . . ' Annabel swallowed, her eyes stinging with sudden tears. 'I didn't know what to think. I saw a picture of the two of you in a cutting at Chantal's. I saw you with Yvette the day you said you went to Milan. Yvette's name was mentioned in connection with yours. Every time I turned round, she was there, at the hotel, the casino . . . '

As her words trailed off, Alain sucked in a breath and sat down on the settee.

'Ah, if you knew the kind of person that she was.'

'That's just it, I don't know. When I asked you, you wouldn't explain.'

'I told you she was of no concern. I hoped you had faith in me.'

She was relieved when the spark of anger left his eyes, but worried at the weary defeat that replaced it. A traitorous part of her that still clung to fairy tales and princes began to hope and dream once more.

'Alain?'

He dragged the fingers of one hand through his tousled hair, then rested his elbows on his knees.

'I will say this about Yvette, and then I do not want to speak of her again. You agree?'

'Yes,' she whispered.

'Yvette Lachaud was the final straw that drove me from tennis. She is an unsuccessful model, beautiful on the surface until you see the coldness in her eyes and discover it goes all the way to her heart.' He sighed and ran a hand over his stubbled jaw. 'We met when I was doing a charity fashion show. Yvette was modelling one of Chantal's dresses, and we were photographed together, hence the cutting you saw.

'That is the only occasion on which we were photographed. I can only assume the photograph you saw was a print she had from that night. It was certainly not placed on my desk by me.

'I went out with her one time, that is all. I went out with many women, chérie, you know that, but it was not serious. I never thought of Yvette again, was not interested in her.'

Annabel watched in silence as Alain rose to his feet and walked towards the window, staring out for several moments before he turned back to her.

'Yvette was obsessed. She followed me around, came to tennis, appeared at the same parties, befriended my friends. She made my life a misery. She found out about me, sold stories to the Press, passed the rumour around that we were a couple.

'My family was pestered. I had enough. Already I was disenchanted with tennis, had made my success, had too much money, and if putting up with people like Yvette was the price, I was not prepared to pay it.

'Now and again, when I think at last I am rid of her, that she was really only interested in me because of the limelight, she turns up again. I do not know how she came to be inside the villa, but it was staged for your benefit with a disregard for the hurt she would cause you, or me.'

Annabel sank on to the edge of the chair opposite him as he returned to the settee.

'But why? What was the point?'

'To make you leave, as she succeeded in doing.'

He shook his head as she looked at him in confusion.

'Can you imagine at all, ma chére, what it is like to be recognised, to live with an old reputation, to have a woman such as Yvette haunting you? The money and the notoriety attract some people. They are not interested in me as a person, do not know me as a man.

'Then I met you, Annabel,' he told her, his voice soft and warm. 'You were fresh, sincere and innocent. You saw me for myself, not the person I was once imagined to be. You did not see only what I could do for you, or buy you,

178

you were not interested in being seen with me for what that might do for you.

'For almost the first time I remember, I was just Alain.' He spread his hands and gave a Gallic shrug. 'Together we were enjoying each other's company, building an understanding. At least, that is what I thought. I could not believe it when Yvette turned up. I did see her when I came back from Milan, but only to tell her for a final time to leave me alone.

'For the first time I cared about someone and instead of being irritated by Yvette's obsession, I was frightened she would ruin this for me.'

He looked at her with heartbreaking vulnerability.

'You must decide whether you believe me or not.'

In her heart, Annabel knew he was telling the truth. He was right. She had come to know him in the week they had been together, and she should have trusted that. It was her own lack of confidence, her belief that it was all too good to be true, that allowed her doubts and Yvette's lies to convince her.

'I do believe you, Alain,' she whispered. 'I'm sorry that my lack of trust hurt you.'

'Chérie — '

'No, wait.' It was her turn to rise to her feet and pace the room as she sought the words she needed to say. 'It is about me not trusting me.'

'Annabel,' he murmured softly, his eyes warm and gentle when she looked at him. 'Come here.'

She did as he requested and allowed him to draw her down beside him, his nearness having the inevitable effect on her senses. He took her hand, linking his fingers with hers.

'It was like a fairytale, Alain — you, Monaco, what was happening between us. I knew it would have to end, and any minute I expected to wake up and find I was dreaming.' She struggled to concentrate as Alain's thumb began to trace across her palm.

'I had never been out with anyone

but Robbie. I loved him and was devastated when he died, but the things I felt with you ... Well, I was frightened. It all happened so fast. I did have doubts and questions about Yvette, and I couldn't believe you were really interested in me. I told myself you were being kind and hospitable because you felt responsible. You'd already offered your help.'

'Chérie,' he chastised, slipping his arm around her shoulders and holding her against him. 'I thought I had shown you in so many ways that you are special and beautiful. How can you doubt it?

'Annabel, it happened very fast, this connection between us, but does that mean the feelings are less real? Is there a time scale for falling in love? I agree that I was foolish not to have explained about Yvette, and I should not have risked what was between us by keeping it from you. For that I am sorry. I will deal with the matter with my solicitor.'

Annabel sighed and snuggled against him.

'I feel sorry for her in a way. It's sad that she has to do this.'

'Do not waste your sympathy. If she cared about me at all, she would not have done so many things to hurt me, have been so spiteful to those I care about.'

His fingers trailed along her cheek as he turned her face up to his.

'Like you, chérie. You have touched my heart and my soul in a way I never dreamed was possible. I was disenchanted, and you healed me, gave me something I have never had before. I want for us always to be together, with no shadows from the past.'

'Alain . . . '

'You think I do not know my own mind?' he teased, humour back in the dark eyes as he watched her changing expressions.

'No. I mean, I'm sure you do.' She broke off and bit her lip. 'Oh, Alain . . . '

182

'It is scary, no, to lose yourself so completely in another person?' His fingertips traced the outline of her lips, his dark eyes smoky. 'We shall have to help each other.'

Annabel smiled, trying to absorb all that he had said, trying to convince herself this was real, that Alain cared for her.

'I have never told another woman that I loved her, have never even thought to ask another woman to marry me. But, Annabel . . . Look at me,' he instructed huskily, his voice sending shivers down her spine. 'I love you, I want you to be my wife.' As tears sprang to her eyes, he went on, 'You take the time you need to feel right. But if what Yvette did made you so sad, then perhaps you love me just a little already?'

'No, Alain.'

'No?'

He looked so crestfallen, so vulnerable, that she smiled, her heart filled with emotion. She twisted in his arms and reached up to kiss him.

'No, Alain,' she murmured against his lips. 'I love you far more than a little.'

For a long time she was lost in the magic of the way he made her feel. She welcomed his kiss with all the love and happiness she thought would be denied her, holding him tight, breathing in his scent, wanting nothing to ever part them again.

Finally, Alain drew back.

'That first night I looked at you, chérie, so vulnerable and beautiful in sleep, I knew,' he admitted.

'You came to my room.'

'Yes.' He chuckled. 'And you heard me talking to myself! I was glad you did not understand French!'

'What was it you said? You never did tell me,' she murmured, looking up at his handsome, smiling face.

'I was asking what was the matter with me!' he confessed with a wry laugh, his fingers exploring the curve of her jaw, the outline of her well-kissed mouth. 'In the twinkling of an eye, I had fallen head over heels in love.'

★   ★   ★

It was exactly a year ago that Annabel had first stood on this balcony and savoured the breathtaking view. And what a year it had been.

At one time, she had never expected to see Monaco or this villa again. And never, in even her most secret dreams, had she believed she would return as Madam Ducret! But here she was, home in Monaco, the place where her own fairytale had come true.

Neither she nor Alain had wanted to wait, and the hastily arranged wedding had run without a hitch. Nor had she wanted an exotic honeymoon in the Caribbean or the Far East, when her only desire had been — and still remained — to be here, in this special place, with Alain.

Over the months of their marriage, she had learned all about the foundation

Alain headed, and she had worked with enthusiasm by his side, humbled and rewarded by the children and what was achieved.

She had even managed to convince Alain to write his long overdue and eagerly awaited autobiography. He had agreed only when she had suggested he donate the income and use the publicity to aid the foundation.

She had been accepted into Alain's family with warmth and love, feeling instantly part of them. And Cecile had welcomed her with open arms, her reaction to the marriage of her beloved Alain warm and enthusiastic. She remained a loyal and loved member of the household.

Secure in the knowledge of Alain's love, Yvette had ceased to matter. True to his word, Alain had taken steps to stop her from pestering them, and with their marriage, the fight had gone out of the other woman.

Annabel did not tell Alain, but her moments of sympathy for Yvette, and her obsession, remained. Now, she had vanished from their lives. Neither her, nor the past could ever spoil their future.

The only setback had been her continued frustration with the French language. Alain had been teaching her with infinite patience, but they were usually sidetracked, especially when it became necessary for him to explain to her again — a spark of roguish laughter in his dark eyes — about masculine and feminine.

A grin curved her mouth. Alain was so good at explaining! Secretly, she hoped that her lessons would last a lifetime.

Hearing a soft footfall behind her, Annabel glanced over her shoulder and smiled as Alain crossed the pink bedroom to the balcony. He looked gorgeous.

The sight of him never failed to stir her blood. She had wondered once if he were a rogue or a gentleman, and she had discovered with delight that he was an exciting and endearing combination of the two.

'What are you doing out here, my dearest?' he asked as he slid his arms around her.

Annabel leaned back into his loving embrace.

'Thinking, remembering, giving thanks.'

Alain rested his chin on the top of her head, and together they looked at the view. Within the sheltering guard of the mountains, and with the shimmering blue-green waters of the Mediterranean caressing the shore, the Principality of Monaco basked in the sunshine.

Sam and her husband had been out for Easter, and in another few weeks, Annabel's parents would arrive. She sighed with contentment. She had never imagined she could be so happy, so much at peace.

Alain slipped his hands over her baggy T-shirt and rested them on her swelling stomach. A chuckle rumbled from his chest as their first child kicked impatiently.

'You wait another month, little one,' he whispered.

Annabel turned round, warmed right through by the hungry fire that never ceased to burn in Alain's dark eyes. She ran a hand across his stubbled jaw and smiled up at him.

'Are you done?'

He nodded.

'For better or worse, the manuscript is on its way to the publishers.'

'I'm proud of you. I know how you struggled with the decision whether to write it or not, but it will be worth it, you'll see.' She melted into a lingering kiss and had to wait several moments before she could ask her next question. 'Did you come up with a title in the end?'

'It was easy.' He grinned.

'So tell me, don't tease!'

Alain cupped her face, watching her for a moment before he drew her tightly to him.

'I was sitting there writing about past years with tennis, and I realised that none of the titles, the prizes, the money, meant anything at all . . . not compared to winning your love.'

'Alain — '

'When I wrote about the present and the future, about you, us, what we have together, it became obvious to me.' He looked down at her, the emotions in his heart and soul shining in his eyes, mirroring hers. 'In life and in love, chérie, you are my perfect match.'

THE END

VISIONS OF THE HEART

Christine Briscomb

When property developer Connor Grant contracted Natalie Jensen to landscape the grounds of his large country house near Ashley in South Australia, she was ecstatic. But then she discovered he was acquiring — and ripping apart — great swathes of the town. Her own mother's house and the hall where the drama group met were two of his targets. Natalie was desperate to stop Connor's plans — but she also had to fight the powerful attraction flowing between them.